The Book of Benny Wu

First Edition: 09/2014
Printed in the United States of America
ISBN: 0692362819

Contents

There are a few people I have to thank Christie Nisch, Tiffany Mitchell, Kimberly Window Giles, Hortense Johnson, Nikki Lemon, Juan Jasso, Kiera Griffin, Lucia Brown, Marilyn Davenport, Robyn Campbell, Alethea J Brown, DJ Lay, the beautiful Nana and my father pro tem Benny Booker.

*This book, as with everything I do,
I do for Nail*

The Book of Benny Wu

By
Andre' Giden

She's been my inspiration
Showed appreciation
For the love I gave her through the years
Like a sweet magnolia tree
My love blossomed tenderly
My life grew sweeter through the years

~ Stevie Wonder ~

CHAPTER 1

"Fathers provoke not your children to do evil."

Marcus's mother could not pick a good man if good men were all she had to pick from. His father did not even stick around long enough to find out she was pregnant. Marcus never knew him, and David, his mother's first boyfriend, he could remember, made it clear. There is a difference between a "David" and a "Daddy." Daddies go out into the world and bring it back for their kids; use love to measure their discipline. David would get mad whenever he saw the boy eating anything, and his discipline had no measure. Marcus was small, but he was smart. He learned to steal into the refrigerator at night. It was a lot less stressful on his tiny frame. He was so small that his nightshirt, a white t-shirt, hung off him, swallowing him completely. With his nearly nonexistent, skinny legs; the bleached white cotton seemed to float, through the dark house at night.

That is how he got his name "White Ghost." Once, David woke up drunk and high and saw Marcus flying from the kitchen, and thought he was a ghost. He was so frightened that he jumped through the bay window out front. He started calling Marcus "White Ghost," and it stuck.

A name is important. It helps to define a person, setting them on the path to who they will be. Someone meets a guy named Mark, and it surprises them how much he is like another Mark they know. You meet a black guy named Eddie you would be a little disappointed if he weren't funny. As you grow, people treat you like everyone else with the same name. It helps to program you. That is why you have never met a child named Iblis.

The name fit Marcus, he was White Ghost. All his life he had been a little white ghost, just a blip, a phantom of someone's afterthought.

The saying use to go, children were to be seen and not heard, but White Ghost had learned to be so quiet, so still, like furniture, they would forget he was in the room - be startled when he moved. Like a ghost, people would say things in front of him as if he was partly there, and his knowledge of them had no bearing on the physical world. So when his stepfather, the Reverend Theodore Barrymore, came barreling down the hall with his well-manicured speech about it being "better for a man to marry than to burn," the only part that was shocking was that his mother had only been dead three months.

The A/C kicked on, and Ghost thought, 'Wow.' He had heard of people not letting the body get cold before they find someone else. The boy's mother died the first of May. It was the end of August in Texas; literally, her body was still warm in the grave.

With all of that, Ghost was still, in some way, relieved. Barry that's what everyone called his stepfather, used a clothes hanger to poke holes in the sheetrock along, the baseboards of the wall between their rooms. From which he would watch Ghost with his girlfriend. They would hear him fumbling about in his closet, which lay behind the wall that faced Ghost's bed.

They laughed about it, about him, and Ghost knew the idea of a preacher lustfully watching turned her on. Now, with the introduction of a mystery woman, however, poor the taste of his timing, at least clarified for Ghost who Barry had been watching.

However, that was not a reprieve. Ghost loathed his stepfather. Even before his mother passed, he could not stand the man. He was vile, even if you stripped away the hypocrisy of preaching the evils of pornography while drilling peepholes in the walls. Marcus knew Barry never loved his mother. Worse, she was duped by a simpleton. There was a country charm about him, but in truth, Barry was slow and dull-witted.

Still, none of that mattered. Barry was a grown man, and Ghost, at sixteen, was grown enough not to care what grown people did. His only concern was where they would be doing it.

"What do you mean?" Barry asked.
Benny Wu came charging out of the kitchen, echoing Barry's question, "What he mean?" Barry was unaware that Benny Wu was in the house; he jumped a bit at the sound of his voice, "Forget what he means. You heard what he said,"

Benny Wu continued. "Where are you and the trifling tramp going to live?" His unrelenting gaze caused

Barry to pause.

"Not that I have to explain myself to either of you." Barry countered; his voice wavering a bit. Then he tried to do exactly that, explain. Benny Wu and Marcus were best friends, but Benny wasn't like Ghost.

People that openly buck the law in Texas are called fools. Benny Wu was a damn fool. But place his temperament aside he was streetwise, and despite his mother issues, he was book smart. The State of Texas executed his father when he was eleven leaving him to raise himself. He had seen everything that life vomits. Barry was cautious and rightfully so.

"Brenda Fay left this house to me," Barry roared.

Brenda Fay, like most of us, was trying to fix something that wasn't broken. With what she was given, she had done a great job. She was seventeen when her mother died, and left her with the house, unpaid for, and with a child to raise. Her son was seventeen now, nearly a man, and the house paid off - even if she had caught most of the first notes on her back, and that was her point of pain.

Brenda Fay flew the flag of independence and told herself each time some bastard was sweating his blubbery way to satisfaction on top of her; she was doing what she had to do. However necessary, it left her feeling empty and alone. Being that for so long, she became desperate.

That is what made it so perfect, made him so perfect. She would make up for all her sins in one fell swoop. She would marry a preacher. She would be a preacher's wife. For the first time in her eyes, she would be a respected woman. She did not love him, but that was okay, she would learn too. Many marriages are arranged she rationalized, believing that marriage was more about the commitment than the love. If he could make a commitment to God, whom he could not even see, then, she felt confident; he could commit to her. Not loving him made no difference; she knew how to make him love her.

Preacher, teacher, ditch diggers or doctors all men are the same under the collar, and she was easy to look at. She was cut from a different cloth, and time didn't even look her way. But that wasn't her selling point. It was her house. It was just as beautiful. It was brick; it was paid off, and it set in the middle of Acres Homes.

They call Acres Homes "The 44." With the exception of Watts, you cannot find a larger concentration of poor "and" "or" working class black folks in America, and Preaching, like most other businesses, is all about location.

"She made it "life" property," Ghost reminded him, which meant Barry could stay there as long as he lived, but she had left everything to her son.

"So what are you saying, you gonna kill me?"

"If that's what it takes!" Benny Wu chimed in and crossed the living room to confront Barry face to face. Ghost stepped in between them.

"No, that is not what I'm saying." Ghost interrupted. Then, turning to Barry, he continued, "I am saying my mother expected you to do the right thing. I don't mean any disrespect, but I know my Mama, she would not be happy with you bringing some woman up in her house...not like this."

"To what lady are you referring? I had no particular person in mind. I was just bringing up the fact that I am a-"

"You a lying-!" Benny interjected.

"Wait, Bennie; this ain't got nothing' to do with

you." Ghost turned to Barry, "I am going to take this fool home, and then we'll talk when I get back."

Ghost dropped off Benny Wu and shot down TC Jester to the 610 freeway. When he needed to think, or wanted to drive, he would jump on the freeway and 'surf the loop.'

Normally, he would circle the city until things made sense and became clear. Today, he was afraid he was going to loop Houston like a hula hoop. As he rounded 610 North to 610 East headed towards the Galleria he hit "Open My Heart" by Yolanda Adams; it was his thinking song.

As much as he hated it, Benny Wu was right. Barry was a liar, and the pervert was trying to take his mother's house. Barry had been talking to that girl. Ghost had heard them on the phone several times. Barry had been looking at that tramp even before his mother died. Ghost heard him say so.

It was sunset about a month ago; Ghost and Brenda Fay's favorite time of day. They would sit on the back porch and talk. Most parents and children don't, but it had been just the two of them for so long. There was no doubt Brenda Fay loved her son, and she wouldn't hesitate in her own words to, "whip that ass till it roped like okra" if she thought he needed it. But all in all, they were friends. She had only been gone a little over a month. Missing her, he did what they routinely did. He made a glass of lemonade and thought he would sit on the porch and watch the sun dip behind the fence. As he approached the glass back door, he couldn't see Barry nor could Barry see the door. But what he heard stopped him dead in his tracks. He heard the word "Pretty."

A man without a woman, wife, or daughter could go

forever without saying the word "pretty." In every-day conversation, seldom are men inspired to use that word. With his mama gone, Ghost thought he would never hear that word in that house again. So when he heard it coming from Barry's crusty, country lips, he was stunned. He neither went backward nor forward. He did not squat, nor turn his head. He froze, exactly where he was. He stopped so fast and stood so still even the ice in his glass did not move, and he listened.

"...made it hard for me to concentrate... s.e.r.i.o.u.s... I am serious girl; you put me to mind of that Erica... Badu...I could tell the way you were dressed; she was an influence on you...Gone on...You were getting jealous?. Girl, you stop playing now...Well, who knows maybe next time you be the one to win the brass ring... ha-ha...you know a man needs help in the ministry, and a minister needs help with his man...Ha, ha, ha..."

Ghost almost threw up then, when he heard him say it. Driving around the city now, thinking about it, he was nearly as nauseous. That was probably the same BS he fed his mother.

"Lord Jesus," he thought. If his mother knew, she would flip... In her... gra... He didn't get to finish his thought before he was hitting the blinker, darting for the 288 entrance. He had it. The preacher is gone. He punched it; the big 350 roared, and he shot across two lanes, cutting off a Hispanic guy in a Mustang. He was going to miss the truck. Barry had given it to him but..."Shiiit!" he thought, "Barry signed the title, but we haven't changed it over yet." As far as Ghost was concerned, he could take the truck and whatever he came with, but his time was up. He floored it down 45. He had to get back to Acres Homes as fast as possible.

Acres Homes is like no neighborhood anywhere. Its unusually dense concentration of black folk aside, Acres Homes features another peculiarity.

It is one of the few places where multi-millionaires live next door to people too poor to qualify for welfare. The black folks who originally chartered Acres Homes envisioned a community of self-reliant black folks. Each home sat on no less than one acre, thus the name. It was because, back then; an acre was considered enough land to support a family, who would work the land to feed themselves and to make a living. Most plots were five acres or more.

A stone's throw from slavery chronologically, most folks knew the importance of holding on to the land. In 1967 when the city of Houston annexed Acres Homes, the value of the land went through the roof. What you had was a bunch of black folk with a bunch of land fifteen minutes from downtown Houston, Texas. Once having been considered "the country," Acres Homes was established without deed restrictions. So, people did some of everything with the land. Some broke it up and sold it. Some built apartment complexes and others-built businesses to support the new growth. Some held on to what they had.

They held on even if it meant that, on a chunk of land large enough to land a plane, they had a house in such despair it was amazing that it stood up against the weight of the sun, let alone the force of the wind. Then there were the children like Brenda Fay, who held on and invested in the land their parents left them. Before his death, her father had used the land as collateral to build the new house. Nine years after it was finished her father died. Four years later her mother died. Despite all that, wilding out and getting pregnant; she finished nursing school. Now, after working nearly fifteen years in the medical center, the property was sprawling. If her father, who had built an impressive residence even by today's standards, saw the massive home his daughter had transformed it into, he would not recognize it. More than likely, he would mistake it for the house of a senator.

Brenda Fay overcompensated for her feeling of low self-worth by pouring everything into her home. After she had done everything that she could think to do to the house - including adding a pool, pool house, and a gazebo - then she had a massive brick wall built at the entrance of the property. That wall cost more than most of the houses in Acres Homes. She spent fifteen thousand dollars on the landscape alone. The wall stood 18 feet high, was made of red brick, and, unlike most walls that run straight, it was designed with waves, because of her profound distaste of monotony. Creating what looked more like an entrance to a gated community.

Driving up to it, Ghost knew he could finally get Barry out.

However, as he pulled through the gate, his elation was replaced by a sinking feeling in the pit of his stomach. It had nothing to do with Denny Ray's car parked in the driveway. He didn't even notice it until he rounded the corner of the house. When he saw it, he felt a bit of relief because of all Ghosts' friends; Denny Ray was the nicest.

Now, you can't choose your family. Denny Ray was a Scott, which meant he was born into one of the most-notorious drug families in Texas. But he was a straight kid. Living down the street, from each other, Ghost and Denny

Ray had known each other nearly their entire lives. He was sure Lil Eggy, Edward Muggings, would be inside as well. Unless you caught one of them coming out of the restroom, it was nearly impossible to see them apart. They were so inseparable; most people thought of them as one person, or at least as brothers. Invite one the other will be there as well. Ghost thought it was odd the way Lil Eggy latched on to Denny Ray, but Eggy was in foster care and didn't have a family.

Ghost's anxiety began to wane. He jumped from the truck and walked toward the door. He was shocked when he saw Benny Wu shooting out of it. Bennie's face twisted into an apology; he raised his hands to stop Ghost from going into the house.

"Look, Ghost before you go to trippin.'" There was blood smeared across his knuckles. The sight of the blood rang in Ghost's head so loud that he could not hear Benny saying, "...let me tell you what happen'!" He pushed past him, running into the house. Barry was sitting in a chair in the middle of the kitchen with his hands taped behind his back. His head was cocked to one side. He was a bloody mess.

Benny Wu charged in behind him. Barry squinted trying to clear the blood from his eyes; he blew a blood bubble trying to speak or breathe. It was hard to tell; no sound came out. The horror of the scene moved Benny to explain, "I swear dude, I just three pieced him."

That was the truth; he just hit him three times, but the first and third found the same place on his face above his right eye. Now it lay open like someone peeled back two inches of his forehead and found a stash of cottage cheese. Not to be outdone, the second had performed similarly, on the other side of his face, leaving his jaw with a gratuitous vent just below his cheekbone.

Sometimes it can be a bit confusing when people speak. That is because two things are being transmitted simultaneously: There is what they said and just beneath that is what they meant. What Marcus said was, "What have you done?" What he meant was, "How could you do this?"

Benny Wu's answer satisfied neither. "I was just going to talk to him!" he insisted, raising his bloody hands, palms open and forward, in a posture of both denial and defense.

Marcus grabbed a knife off the counter and began cutting the tape from his hands. "Then why is he taped up?"

"How else was I going to stop him from running to the laws after I done whipped his ass like this?"

As odd as it sounded, that was the only thing that made any sense. Benny Wu went on to explain how he was just supposed to scare him, "but he studded up and swung!"

That wasn't altogether true. Barry didn't get to swing. Instead, he started spouting at Benny Wu that it was his house and, 'wasn't nobody gone make him leave.' He went into a rant. He would marry whom he wanted; when he wanted, and in the meantime, he was going to bring whomever, he wanted 'up and through there.'

And when he had built his confidence up enough, he tried to shine. He decided to take him a shot, but he didn't get to swing. By the time he drew his fist and cocked it, Benny Wu had already hit him twice. Benny Wu swung when he saw the gilt and had knocked him out before he even started bleeding. More to his defense than to his credit, it was reflex. He had chopped Barry up before he knew what he had done, but those words, however remorseful, fell

11

on deaf ears.

All Ghost could think was, "This was so unnecessary." He was going to call the police; tell them Barry had been watching him from those holes he made in his closet.

Barry was regaining consciousness, but his ears had not caught up with time. His delirium combined with the confusion of focusing through a haze of blood, he thought he was alone. His mind numb with pain, he thought he was thinking to himself, but he said out loud, "Pull ...together, get the law...Got him..."

Ghost barked, "Man ya'll help me; we got to get this fool to the hospital!" to Benny Wu and to the rest of them, realizing for the first time that there were others in the room. Besides Denny Ray, who was in the corner looking horrified there was Lil Eggy, sitting there eating a sandwich surprisingly, unmoved.

Ghost began to cut the tape from Barry's leg. As it swung free, Barry muttered, "Yeah officer, I want to press charges."

Concerned for them both, Benny Wu added nervously, "Lord, this motherfucker is delirious."

"Eggy!" Ghost called out. It was the first time he had addressed him directly, "Get something to help me clean this man up."

One of the things that foster care teaches is pecking order; Lil' Eggy snapped to attention. Looking up from his sandwich, he moved swiftly towards the paper towels.

"Bastard gone be mad at somebody..." Barry muttered, "...suppose to be mad at his dumb ass Mama..."

Maybe it was the word bastard, or it could have been calling the young man's recently departed mother a dumb ass.

Perhaps he had just grown tired of preachers and their self-righteous indignations. Whatever it was, like the levy in New Orleans, the youngster couldn't hold anymore. He broke.

Benny Wu had seen it happen so many times. His mother was bipolar, back when it was just called crazy. So he recognized it immediately. That blink then flash, where the eyes of a sane person closes, then opens the intent gaze of a lunatic.

Benny recognized the look immediately and lunged for Ghost, tackling him to the floor, but he was too late. The knife was already six inches in Barry's chest.

There was a loud sucking sound as Barry tried to breathe, but it quieted as his lungs began to fill with his blood. He gasped, and then it gurgled from his mouth. Lil Eggy looked at the wad of paper towels in his hands and said, "we gone need mo' than this."

CHAPTER 2

"Evil is a greedy beast that will grow as long as it is fed."

Marcus looked at Bennie. Then he looked at Barry and back again. His eyes screamed, "What have I done!" Benny answered in gesture and started to clean up the mess.

He called to Denny Ray. He wasn't worried about Eggy. In some ways, they were alike, and he knew the youngster would take it to the grave. But Denny Ray, even with Barry sitting there bleeding like a stuck pig, Denny Ray was the biggest mess in the room. He was on the verge of a conniption. He was standing there with his mouth twisted open, but there was no sound. It was as if he was trying to scream inwards. He put his hands over his mouth as if he was afraid of what might come out, and then he started bouncing up and down, fanning his hands all the time his eyes buck wide... Benny Wu grabbed him and shook him a bit, then looked him in the eyes.

More murderers are executed in the great state of Texas, than any state in the Union. President Bush when he was Governor of Texas set in a policy to fast-track the appeal process. When asked why he said, "In Texas, we fatten up steers not death row inmates." The solution to over scheduling issues was a double bed. Bottom line no matter how horrified a person may be when it comes to murder in Texas, it doesn't make a difference how scared a person gets, they do not tell on themselves. Not in Texas!

"Okay, this is deep Denny... Now, I'll take this body, and any heat that goes with that, but I need to know that once I leave here can't nobody tell it. I need to know you are going to keep your mouth shut."

"I ain't-."

Benny Wu cutting him off, "That ain't good enough," and he pulled the knife from Barry's body. His body began to twitch, and his eyes started to flutter.

"Benny naw... Naw ...Naw ...Naw Bennie"

"Naw Benny my ass. I love you bruh, but right now either I can trust you or I can't." Denny Ray shook his head as Benny Wu put the knife in his hand, "Denny Ray, either I can love you or I can't."

Denny Ray was scared because he knew that Benny Wu was serious. Either he was going to cut the preacher or he was going to have to cut Benny Wu.

Barry gasped loudly.

Benny Wu urged, "You need to hurry. Are you in or out?"

He searched every part of his mind, going memory by memory for an answer. He went through church and schools but could find nothing. He thought about Ms. Kolas; she had been his ninth-grade counselor. Odd shaped woman, who during orientation gave a moving speech about peer-pressure. She did not cover this. He stopped thinking, closed his eyes and pushed the knife into the preacher's gut. His body so relaxed the knife sunk to the handle. Blood and bile squirted onto Denny Ray's hand. He pulled out the bloody knife, mortified. His eyes now fixed on his hand drenched in blood. "My God," he thought, "the blood."

Lil Eggy ran over and grabbed the knife from Denny Ray's hand and in a singular motion as if he had something to prove swung, like a Karate chop, "EeeYAA" plunging the knife between the neck and shoulder. He swung with such voracity Benny Wu's face conveyed that he didn't know how to take it.

"I don't want nobody thinking it's nothing punk about me!" He looked back at Denny Ray, who was still staring at his bloody hands- transfixed.

"Fuck you Eggy!" Denny Ray shouted, "It's a man dead, up in here."

"Fuck that man! Bruh' you heard what Benny said...this is his; we don't never have to say nothing about this ever again, we weren't ever here."

"Denny Ray, you know my word is bond," Benny Wu reassured him, but Denny Ray could not get past Lil Eggy acting as if Barry had just lost on the PlayStation.

"It's a man dead, up in here." He repeated.

Lil Eggy held up his hand and then started counting, "4...5...6. There you go every six seconds a child in Africa dies of Malaria that don't have shit to do with us either. People die all the time. That's not our fault. Believe me, Bruh, it's nothing you can do about people dying. You can wake up one morning in a hospital to find out some drunk ass Mexican, who wasn't even supposed to be here done killed everybody in your family."

No one saw Ghost leave to go to the garage so when he came busting in the back door with the tarpaulin, he scared the hell out of everybody. Denny Ray grabbed his chest like he was having a heart attack and screamed almost as loud as Benny Wu. Lil Eggy took off running. He shot straight through the den and was about to run into the living room.

The living room had been Brenda Fay's favorite room. One day she went into Canton's in the Galleria, where she saw a white sofa with crystal feet. She thought it was the most beautiful thing that she had ever seen, so she bought it and every piece that went with it. Then she bought white carpet to set them on; the combination was so brilliant it seemed electric. Before she knew it, she had done the entire room in white. She added a few splashes of blue and sea-foam green, but mostly everything was white, even the vacuum cleaner, which was for cleaning that room only.

Brenda Fay was so meticulous; to her, this was the most comfortable place in the house because she could ensure that it was pristine at a glance, and she found that relaxing.

Now, Lil Eggy was charging towards his mother's room with blood on his feet. Ghost screamed, "Eggy, the carpet!"

He snapped and tried to stop, but the momentum was too great. He slid a bit and looked like a wide receiver trying to keep both his feet inbound. There was not much he could do; he was going to hit that carpet. It was unavoidable. However, years of foster living had given him advance skills in "leaving folks stuff alone." As he was falling, he flipped over so that he landed on his back with his feet in the air.

Ghost took off Lil Eggy's shoes and then he helped him to his feet.

Ghost said, "Look, from this moment on we need to be very careful. We have all watched CSI; we cannot leave any evidence." And they were.

First, Ghost went into his mother's old meds and broke Denny Ray off a half a Xanax and poured him a Grey Goose on ice. He had seen that concoction pull magic out of his mother's mood.

Benny Wu and Lil Eggy took care of the body. They laid the body on the tarpaulin. They grabbed the corners and dragged it out back to the pool house. It was an old Jim Walter's straight frame house that sat near the rear of the property when Marcus's grandfather bought it. They lived in it until the new house was built in the front of it. His grandfather didn't want it to live in, but it sat on a slab, so he didn't tare it down. Instead, he used it for storage.

Naturally, his mother went the other way. After Anthony and Sylvan had installed the pool, she had them completely remodel the house. Taking out the front door and the wall of what was the living room transforming it into an open cabana style area where they could sit and enjoy the pool in the complete shade. The layout was the same as it had been as a home. There was a large sitting area. Straight back was the dining room where she added a large bay window which wrapped around the back corner rounding into the kitchen. She insisted on the double-paned tempered glass. Her love was for the sunlight, and as long as there was any light, it spilled through the kitchen and washed through the living room. The back door was replaced with a sliding door that was the true charm of the pool house, when they were opened, it forced whatever breeze there was through. However, it is not uncommon to have a day in Texas where it is a hundred degrees in the shade with the wind as flat as the land. Preparing for that inevitability, the bedrooms were left closed off and air-conditioned. The windows on the pool side were replaced with sliding glass doors the rooms were also accessible from the back hallway that led to the restrooms. That's the way they dragged the body.

Surprisingly from the knife, there wasn't much blood. Ghost's wound was the fatal blow. It landed high in his chest, piercing both his lungs. They filled with blood, and he slowly drowned on that. Most of the bleeding was internal, but that was about to change. Benny Wu got another knife from the kitchen. Then he and Lil Eggy put the body in the tub and ghoulishly performed the necessary task of cutting it up.

Everything was moving fast. Benny Wu felt like he was in one of those movies, traveling at warp speed, moving so fast light can't keep up. Only it's was Bennie's actions they had not caught up to his common sense. Leaving stretched out like lagging beams of light fear, dread and a host of other emotions. However, when he started down the driveway in that truck, with that chopped up body in the back they did, and he jammed on the breaks. For a moment, he sat there, like he was taking his driving test. With his hands at ten and two; gripping the wheel.

He looked in the rearview and saw the guys watching him not drive off. Flooded with emotions, staring at the huge wrought iron gate and rolling brick fence, he had the strangest thought. He thought about the Hollywood sign. Only he saw the word "Opportunity."

CHAPTER 3

"Success is the love child of preparation and opportunity."

In certain ways, all women are beautiful. Like flowers, they are precious in form and design, and as titillating in their fragility as in their aroma, still, she was uncommon. In a field of bluebonnets, she was a lily, an African Queen. And while they were all of the same hue, in style and shape, she bloomed much higher than the rest. Her petals splashed with color. She greeted the sun with a whole new attitude.

Like Dorothy Dandridge or Elizabeth Taylor, she had that type of beauty it was necessary to use her whole name. Everybody knows a pretty Toni, but if you are talking about Toni Braxton, well... now you are talking about something. Her name was Felicia Gilmore and any man, even a man of the cloth, would have given his rent money, even the rent at the church, to be the mirror she was standing in front of as she slid into her matching Siluga panties.

She smiled a bit when she rubbed her hands across the lace, not because of any school girl vanity. While she recognized she was attractive, she promised never to fall into that trap.

No, she was excited with her purchase. She loved the way they fit and the way the seam disappeared into her skin, the softness and intricacy of the lace. They were the best and that part she loved most of all. She loved the best.

Loving parents, especially if they were of modest means in their youth, work twice as hard to give their children all they never had. Most often, unwittingly robbing them of the one thing they did have, want.

There is no motivator like "want." Felicia's grandmother made the mistake of stealing "want" from Felicia's father. She gave him everything her heart desired. He never knew "want" nor its older brother "need."

Being the Dean of Applied Mathematics at Prairie View A&M University, her grandmother took an analytical approach. She ruined her son by lavishing him with gifts. In rectify, the raising of her granddaughter, a responsibility she genuinely accepted, she did with no pomp. Except for a roof over her head and the barest of essentials, she nearly never bought the child anything.

That lingerie, like everything else she wanted, she got for herself.

Now, normally she would not wear something so nice just to hang out, but this was a special occasion. She wasn't planning anything tawdry. However, it was her belief that true beauty was within and permeated out and nothing destroyed the flow of sexy like itchy drawers.

"You did what!" Ghost bellowed, still dripping wet. After he had cleaned the restroom in the pool house, he took the power washer and filled it with bleach and hot water, and sprayed the whole place down. He was just putting the wet-vac away when Denny Ray walked up, wearing one of his best shirts mind you, and dropped a bombshell on him.

The Xanax, combined with the body being gone, relaxed Denny Ray closer to his normal self. Close enough for him to remember that he had told his girlfriend, Tanasha to come over.

Ghost loved his mother so much that he had a respect that extended to all women, and a strict code of not using derogatory terms against any female. However, he looked his buddy in the eye and said, "This ain't no time for your bitch!"

"Hey, you should never refer to a woman in terms you wouldn't want used for your mother or sister," Denny Ray said jokingly throwing Ghost's rhetoric back in his face.

Ghost completely missed the humor. "Dude; I just sopped up all eight pints of a man's blood, I reiterate…this… Ain't No Time…For your bitch," He looked him in the eyes so that Denny Ray would know that he meant what he had said. Denny Ray nodded slightly Ghost took that as an understanding and started toward the house.

But it wasn't, and Denny Ray said to his back, "I asked her to swing by before you-"

Ghost stopped in his tracks. He turned to Denny Ray and asked, "Before what?"

Denny Ray, trying to keep things light said, "Before things got all busy."

Ghost backed his anger a bit, "Why don't you call her. Tell her to change directions."

"Cause they're here."

"They?!"

Denny Ray points to the gate, through which you could see the car's headlights shining. Ghost looked at himself covered with water, "Man, what the-?"

"Look, you know Tanasha don't drive. She had her cousin Felicia to bring her, and you know Keyanda freak ass gone be with her." Keyanda had a thing for Ghost; Denny Ray thought exploiting that would seal the deal.

He was wrong. Ghost said, "Denny I am not feeling this."

Desperate, Denny Ray dug deep.

"Man, it's gone look messed up if we blow them off all of a sudden: besides we could use the alibi."

Now to Ghost that made plenty of sense, and without even being aware, he was nodding agreeing; Denny Ray took it as a sign he had one more swing.

"Straight love, the house is kept" which meant honestly; the house was clean. "You can run go take a shower. I will hold it down until you get downstairs…Kick it a minute, then boo yow, I make an excuse and drag everybody out of here."

Lil Eggy popped his head out of the backdoor. He also found his way to Ghost's closet. He was decked out. The clothes were falling off of him, but he wore them like he bought them that way. "These girls are at the gate you want me to buzz them in or what?"

"All right, cool… but make it quick because I can't do a bunch of that ki-kiing right now."

"E-Yea" Lil Eggy barked as he popped back into the house.

"We gone keep it a player in and out, and, dude,

Tanasha's cousin is supposed to be premium."

"I already said its cool, you can get off the gas," he said and headed into the house.

Benny Wu slid along on his stomach, dragging a blanket with the Glad trash bag on top of it. He had marveled at the commercial where they put the broken grand piano into one. He didn't know if that claim was true, but one chopped up human, no problem.

He knew where it was supposed to be, but he had never looked for it before. He glided past old faded trash and bottles dirtied by dust and time. There was a doll. For the life of him, he could not understand where that came from. The old deflated football and the plastic rifle he got but the doll. He shined the light over there. Just as he was pulling the light away, he saw it, or what he was sure was it.

The large wrought iron gate swung open, and Felicia pulled through slowly. With all the trees and lights, it felt more like an episode of the Bachelor.

The driveway curved and then widened into an open area so large it was a little confusing to navigate. She slowed as she tried to gain her bearings. Then she noticed the skinny young man, flailing his arms, waving her to a place to park.

Tanasha leaned over into the front seat and said out of the window, "That's my baby." Then she looked her cousin directly in the eyes, with a clear, 'don't make me say it again.'

Felicia smiled to herself. Whenever a woman got jealous started tripping about a man she didn't even know, let alone want, she took it as an acknowledgment of her dominance. It was like bowing before the Queen.

It was a guilty pleasure, but she found it amusing when women acted like dogs, peeing on trees. That is what Keyanda had jumped in her front seat to do. With her Marcus, this and Marcus that. The marking of territory, the mindless chitter chatter it was all bowing.

She was not concerned with this Marcus. She was like everyone else in Acres Homes. She just wanted to see the house. She had passed the magnificent gate so many times, and like everyone else that passed it, wondered about the house. Now true, she was dressed to the nine, but she dressed nicely every day, believing you never get a second chance to make a first impression. And in all sincerity, a gate is like a door; you never know what you may find on the other side.

While she wasn't there to step on any toes, she felt it advantageous to help Keyanda with her confusion. As if she was concerned about her looks, she pulled down the vanity mirror on the driver side to check herself. She grabbed her lipstick, pulled out the applicator and tapped it to her already luscious lips. She turned to Keyanda, who had been watching her like a groupie. When their eyes met, Keyanda became self-conscious and pulled down the vanity mirror on her side. Etched in the glass at the top was the word REMEMBER, and at the bottom, A PIMP IS CHOSEN. Felicia glanced over at Keyanda to see if she got the message. Since she was frowned up, she assumed she did.

"Now we can all get out and enjoy ourselves," she

said as she exited the car. One of her grandmother's mantras was from Proverbs 2 "above all thy getting's, get thee an understanding" and while she disagreed with much about Moma2, she found the Bible to be dead on.

Contrary to belief, it is not hard to kill a person; it's hard to get away with it. Benny Wu crawled from under the house with the blanket and emptied the plastic bag. He placed them in a barrel with Barry's bloodied clothes and the tarp. He doused everything with gasoline and set it on fire. In his zeal, he had poured too much. The flames licked high in the sky, and Benny Wu's confidence rose with them. No one would ever find the preacher.

Just as he had that thought, he saw what he was sure was the police. They were at the end of the street coming his way. Benny Wu fell back on his training.

All higher life forms want to pass on whatever understanding it has to its offspring. In humans, it is as much a part of procreation as insemination. The nefarious are no different. From the time his son first began to read, Benny Wu's father, of the same name, wrote to him from prison. Trying to father from a cell is difficult. His father decided against trying to dispense either love or discipline on paper. Instead, knowing this was all of him his son would ever have, he made him a list of rules and observations, both specific and vague. Those tattered pieces of paper, they were his legacy. With a son's love, he quoted them like they were the Bible, the book of Benny Wu.

Page five, second paragraph reads "the police only notice what is out of place. They have too much to be concerned with to concentrate on what looks completely normal." So even though it was the middle of the night, Benny Wu began to pick up trash in the yard.

In Acres Homes, people burned trash and leaves. They stand around burning barrels drinking. In the winter, the fire chases away the cold, and in the summer, the smoke chases away the mosquitoes.

He had walked over to the barrel two or three times with trash by the time the policeman cruised in front of the house. While it wasn't an everyday occurrence it was commonplace, so the overburdened officer drove right pass.

It was done. Benny wanted to exhale. The body was gone, and no one would ever find it. He stood there looking into the fire, watching the last of the clothes burning. He wanted to feel relieved, but he knew that was the easy part. This is where things could get a little tricky, but he had a long drive ahead of him with plenty of time to get things together.

Tanasha had hopped over Pink and was the first out of the car. Denny Ray began to smile the moment he saw her head pop out of the back. She ran around over to him and gave him a hug. Rising to the tips of her toes tall with long legs, her pelvis pushed against his stomach. Through his shirt, he could feel her heat. He closed his eyes and surrendered to the fantasy as he wrapped his arms around her small frame and pulled her tighter.

He opened his eyes and saw Felicia and let her go. Had Tanasha not been so tall she might have hit the ground.

"Dang," she said as she turned around to see what

his eyes had seen. She punched Denny Ray in the shoulder, "Close your mouth… This is my cousin, Negro, my first cousin Felicia."

He had the same look every man did when they were introduced to her using just her first name. He looked hungry, like what he had just been fed was not enough.

She had seen that look before. She stuck her hand out and said, "Felicia Gilmore." She didn't understand why that helped, but usually, it did.

She did not understand that men tend to be mathematical and beauty can be an illusion. Touching her proved that she was real. He grabbed her hand with both of his, and with eyes wide, "Oh Felicia Gilmore."

See, he knew two Felicias. He needed a specific file name. There was no doubt he would be recalling her form from his memory, and he would need to know exactly where to find her. Not to mention, she was so fine there was the ever-looming threat that she could override his mind and erase the other Felicias from his memory. Whenever anyone would say, "Do you know Felicia," he would automatically think about her. That wouldn't be so bad; he thought if one of those Felicias wasn't his mother. No, she had to-

"Boy! Don't you hear me talking to you" Tanasha shouted cutting through Denny Ray's thought?

Startled back by her yelping, he released the girl's hand.

Ghost reached his hand into the shower and turned it on. He was tired, not physically, but mentally he was spent, spiritually beat, and emotionally drained. Everything he did was deliberate and took great effort , walking, thinking, blinking, even watching.

The water hopped electrically off the marble floor. All that water popping around drops, of all sizes, bouncing at varying heights, it was too much. His mind could not process anymore. Instead, he concentrated on one section by the drain. It was like a finish line. If he could just make it there, he could wash this day away, and be done. He placed his hand in the water to check the temperature and made his move.

He stepped into the warm water. It flowed across his head and down his back. He watched the waterfall off of him and circled down the drain. Then he saw a faint trace of pink. He assumed it was Barry's blood. He had tried to be so careful. He had cleaned like his mother had taught him, with bleach and water, being careful about the blood. He grabbed his Axe shower gel and rubbed it in his head. With his bare hands, he scrubbed his entire body.

Then grabbed the shower head and let the water wash the suds away, but he was afraid to open his eyes. Afraid he would still see blood. He tried to tell himself that he had done what was necessary. Barry was a pervert. He had lied to his mother and had used her. And he was about to steal their house. What he had done was necessary. He squeezed his eyes tight and then burst into tears. He was the pervert; he had bastardized the word. He had twisted everything his mother had ever taught him. He was a thief, and worse what he stole he could never pay back.

CHAPTER 4

"Here comes a bouncing baby boy."

Benny Wu cruised down I-10, but he raced through his plan. He had been to the end and back a hundred times. Step by step. When the amber highway lights of Texas gave way to the dark, and he knew he was in the politically stained state of Louisiana, but he had to get further down the road to be safe. He took the Toomey turn off but would wait until he was on the back side of Vinton before he activated the phone that he bought at Wal-Mart. He only needed two more things; for the country to be the country, and his Uncle Tj to be at home.

Ghost pulled himself together, got up off the floor and got dressed. He threw on a pair of gray camouflage Levis shorts; a t-shirt and some flip-flops; he was not trying to impress anyone. His plan was to go downstairs, say his hellos, and then vamoose.

Denny Ray was true to his word. He did not even bring his guest in the house. They were hanging out by the pool.

Ghost went downstairs. It was dark. The darkness felt like a blanket, warm and safe.

Moving through the shadows, he felt more like himself. Walking past the white room, he recognized the quiet.

Subconsciously, most people are afraid of the absence of sound. Every little lull must be filled with music, laughter or meaningless chatter, but Ghost found immense pleasure in the silence. He walked into the den and on through to the kitchen. Through the window, he could see Denny Ray lounging on a cabana chair, Tanasha lying between his legs. He is chilling' hard Ghost thought. And he was; he looked as if he was on the deck of a cruise ship.

Ghost hated to go out there and bust up his fun, but that was exactly what he was planning to do. Walk out there and bust it up, politely clean house. What he needed was some more of this, a little more solitude, a double helping of this elbow room, with some time to himself on the side.

He turned the knob and opened the door. Tanasha was the only one who noticed him coming out; their eyes met through the glass. She nudged Denny Ray with her elbow.

He was pretending to be engrossed in his conversation with Keyanda, but he was watching, waiting for a glance of Felicia. His leering had become incessant, and Felicia knew her cousin would eventually notice and get upset. To slow him down and avoid confusion, she turned her back to him. Subsequently, Felicia's back was to the door, she didn't see Ghost when he popped out. She didn't see the light that lit in Keyanda's eye and the nervous excitement in her smile, nor from her vantage could she hear

Denny Ray, not that it would have mattered.

"Hey, what's up Ghost? I told everyone bout your headache. We were just going to squat a click and then bounce."

Felicia didn't hear what he had said. What she did notice was a quick quiver in Keyanda's breath. She turned to see what had elicited such a response, and Ghost saw her.

In order to truly understand love at first sight, one has to be a bit of a scientist. It is the only way to grasp the physics of the power of attraction and its effect on space-time. How it makes the impossible possible, like walking into a garden shed, but inside it's the size of the TajMahal.

That is the only way you could understand, how in one moment, a single beat, an infinitesimal fraction of a second, he could see a lifetime with her. Two point five kids, a job at the light company, and a dog named Snickers. If you can perceive time being blown up into a bubble, and normal time having to travel up and around its greasy outer surface, while he zoomed blissfully through its middle. Then you understand how in the exact moment that he looked into her eyes he fell in love. In the same moment, without missing a beat, he turned to Denny Ray and said, "Na, bruh I'm fine. I took a BC before I jumped in the shower" he turned back to Felicia, "I'm good."

The ride back they were both silent. For miles, neither one said a single word. Tj would occasionally glance at Benny Wu, amazed how much his nephew looked like his little brother. Now racing through the dark, driving down the same streets he and his brother drove as young men, seeing some of the same places, it was like being back in time, "Lord, you look like Lil Bennie." Tj said.

Benny Wu had only seen his father three times that he could remember. He looked like an ice cream man in one of those old movies, with his white pants and shirt, black leather belt and shoes, everything pressed perfectly and shiny.

If you are sentenced to death in the great state of Texas, there is only one guaranteed way to stay your execution. Kill someone else. In Texas, no murder goes unanswered. Until they can get a conviction on your new charge, you get a stay. Then they run the sentences concurrently. Unfortunately, you can only execute a man once.

If you are an inmate working on death row, you know to get it right. You know not to play games with the inmates that are on death row. You know to keep your distance, but most important, you know to watch your mouth. Because the man in front of you is sentenced to death and all he needs to do to get an extra six, seven months of life, is open your wise cracking neck.

One inmate nearly decapitated another with the wire from a spiral tablet. That was before Bush, what they on death row call the good old days. He got two and a half extra years because that murder had to be addressed. In Texas, they never close the book on murder. Everything kept coming back to that.

Finally, Benny Wu spoke, "Look, when the law shows up, and Unk, they will show up. Don't add anything. All you know is what I told you."

"I got it, nephew. You know, you are just like your

Daddy... he would say KISS."

"Kiss."

"Yeah kiss, k.i.s.s. Keep it simple, stupid."

Benny chuckled and then said, "No disrespect Unk... But yeah... Let's kiss." They rode the rest of the way in silence.

Ghost did not approach her. He had concealed it well, but he was smitten. The last thing he wanted to do was make one of those boyish mistakes, to say the wrong thing or to be too anxious. He had been caught off guard and needed time to recoup. He decided to take advantage of being on his home field. He instructed Lil Eggy, who was always hungry and ready to eat something, to fire up the barbeque pit. Naturally, he jumped to it, and Ghost disappeared into the kitchen.

The kitchen was one of the places he felt most at home. Being a mama's boy, with no brothers or sisters, he spent as much time in the kitchen with his mother as she did. He was comfortable there. He took the chicken out of the refrigerator, set it in the sink, and began rinsing it when the door opened.

He was not completely ready for his first encounter, so he was relieved when Keyanda bopped in, "What are you cooking?"

"I'm just going to throw this bird on the pit."

That glee was short-lived because Felicia walked in behind Keyanda. Felicia's beauty was already unsettling. Marcus had fallen so deep into her eyes, the boy could see the girl's heart beating, but when she walked through the door, he was done.

Usually, Ghost is hard to read, but his heart was singing like the Rude Boys, and it was written all over his face at least to Keyanda. Feeling a little deflated she moved around the kitchen island.

There were three stools that set under the offside. She pulled out one and took a seat.

"Can I help you?" Felicia asked.

Her voice was extremely confident while soft and sweet. Existentially Ghost could not get pass the idea that the very first thing he ever heard her say was, 'Can I help you' because at the time he had never been more in need.

"Girl, he's not going to let you do nothing," Keyanda added anticipating Felicia's rejection.

"Wait. Who are you?" Ghost asked.
She smiled and stuck out her hand, "Felicia Gilmore" she answered.

He looked at his hands covered in chicken grease and water and through his arms wide open and said: "Act like you love me."

To his dismay, she hugged him. He had thrown his arm out there asking for a hug, but now that her arms were wrapped around him; he felt like Robbie in A Christmas Story, only it was more than finding a BB gun under the tree. He felt there might really be a Santa Claus.

She inhaled as she released him, "You are wearing Usher."

He didn't know how to read her statement. It wasn't his favorite fragrance. His mother fell in love with it. It was growing on him, but he had only started wearing it to finish the bottle.

"It's my every day." Ghost replied.

She could sense his uncertainty, "No, I like it. It's light and clean."

That's what his mother had said when she brought it home. He smiled and thought about how much his mother would have loved her.

Felicia interrupted his thought, "I like a man to smell clean."

"Well, like I said this is my every day." Needless to say, he was glad that he listened to his mother, and always wore cologne.

"I'm White Ghost."

"Why do they call you 'White Ghost,'" she asked.

He wanted to tell her the story, the whole story with all the pain and laughter, not the washed-out version he told everyone else, but with Keyanda sitting there, it seemed like mixed company.

In a half smile, he said instead, "I thought you said you wanted to help."

That cut Keyanda deeper. As many times as she had been to that house, in that kitchen and offered to help, saying the exact same thing, to see Felicia moving towards the sink to peel potatoes was like watching them make out.

CHAPTER 5

"In the kingdom by the sea."

Their attraction was like the Antilles. While they were in the same place experiencing the same warm and passionate breezes, there was a greater and lesser. However, Felicia liked Ghost. She thought he was cool and cute, and she liked the way he moved in the kitchen. He was confident, even the way he held a knife and used it; she thought it was sexy. The way he cut the onions, and celery, even the way he lined the cookie sheet with aluminum foil. She didn't know why he did it to make potato salad, but he didn't fumble about trying to remember where things were or what he was to do next. He moved with precision, and that was indeed sexy. All the time Ghost, who was usually very quiet was laughing and talking. It was effortless which was most impressive to everyone except Keyanda.

Felicia thought he was a bit of a choir boy, but he was handsome in that role. She could not throw stones because she had grown up in the church as well. He was smart and witty and had something to say. Greater, he had that thing that separated boys from men. He knew how to listen. Most boys, some of them grown, spend the majority of their time in conversation trying to think of what to say next, and the rest of the time is spent waiting to say it.

She was tired of guys who pretended to listen. Nodding their heads to everything she said, just going along, saying yes and thinking that one day they might get them some. Ghost listened and made an effort to understand, not just agreed before he had even heard what she said, or thought that he knew better before she even finished her thought. Most women don't get what they want, not because they are not asking, but because they are not being heard. She paid attention to how a man paid attention, and Ghost was paying close. It was refreshing.

In the midst of elation over her prospects, Lil Eggy burst through the door; he was holding a sausage in a pair of tongs.

"Looky here, son!" He was spinning the link in Ghost's face for his examination and approval, "Not poked evenly blistered until it busted." Ghost laughed at Lil Eggy's impersonation. He had been teaching him how to barbeque and was impressed with his pupil.

"Aw, that's nothing Ghost. Wait until you see this chicken!" He said proudly.

"Well, that's what's up." Ghost said smiling at Felicia. He was having so much fun, that he did something they never do in Texas. He had forgotten about the meat. The air was festive, and Felicia was so beautiful it didn't matter. However, everybody was not caught up in the merriment.

When Felicia smiled and said to Ghost, "I am so glad that you are feeling better."

And Ghost replied, "I am glad you are concerned with my feelings." Everybody laughed, except Keyanda.

For her, it wasn't cute. It was like they were fawning over each other. Of course, their touching was incidental and their bumping accidental, but to her, it was groping and grinding, and it was nauseating. In a desperate attempt to get Ghost's attention and remind him that she had known him longer, she called him by his government name.

"Marcus!" She blurted his name out so fast she didn't have time to think of what it was she wanted.

So when he jerked around, and said, "Yeah," she was left standing there with her mouth open looking as stupid as she felt, "Aw, aw…Felicia…wanted to see the house."

Aw, what in the hell did she say that for she thought as Felicia's eyes lit up.

"Wait! You're Marcus?" Felicia said, genuinely surprised because she had no idea that he was the one Keyanda was crushing on. When he came out, to the pool, she didn't say anything. She didn't walk up hug him, or wave, nothing. He didn't throw her an extra anything wink, smile, word or glance; there had been nothing.

Denny Ray had called him Ghost, and he had introduced himself as White Ghost. At the time, it sounded like an old Indian name. Acres Homes is so country some people still have horses. In Acres Homes, there are families like the Bushants who claimed to be descendant of Black Seminole. How was she supposed to know? Even though she had stunted in the car, with the mirror, she told herself that she would not bother with Keyanda's dude, but if this is her Marcus, then all bets were off. Besides if there was something between them, no one went out of his or her way to make it known, and at this point, it was hard for her to put a level on how much she cared.

"I thought you were talking about someone else," Felicia said to Keyanda.

"What?" Ghost said smiling, but sensing there had been a conversation about him. He turned his gaze to Keyanda however he was much more accusatory. Feeling exposed Keyanda cowered inside.

Felicia knew that Keyanda had greatly overstated their relationship. Her first inclination was to throw her under the bus by saying "I thought Y'all were a couple."

Marcus would clarify, "Naw, this is just my homegirl, or worst my road dog."

It is okay to be a dudes 'homegirl' if you both see the relationship as that, but if you are sniffing around with the hots for him just part of the pack. Well then you are a female dog in heat, and Keyanda who once felt like she had a chance could see the collar coming.

Instead, Felicia had sympathy for her and said, "Keyanda was saying that you would show me your place" completely letting her off the leash.

"Hell yeah, you get the grand tour. Give me just a second to finish my potato salad." He pulled the cookie sheet he had lined with foil from out of the freezer.

He had used cold water to cool the potatoes and eggs as much as he could, but they still held a little heat. So after he had mixed his potato salad together, he spread it into the frozen sheet and placed it back into the freezer.

"I leave it in here for about 10 or 20 minutes. I like my potato salad really cold. This way, when I scoop it back into the bowl, I can just throw away the foil, nothing to clean," he explained.

She smiled because she liked her potato salad cold as well. Her grandmother, in her eyes, made the best potato salad in the world. Felicia would sit in front of the TV, watch movies, and eat it like ice cream.

"Me too," she said and looked back at Keyanda and asked her if she wanted to come along.

Keyanda looked at Ghost and said, "I've seen the place" and stood up to leave.

Ghost was unmoved and clearly not bothered, "Cool, it's just the two of us then."

Before he got the whole sentence out of his mouth, they were gone, and Keyanda was still standing there smoothing her clothes.

Since they were standing in the kitchen, he started the tour in reverse, but he still showed the house as his mother would have, careful to point out it's every special point.

After he had been walking and talking for about twenty minutes, he stopped and said, "I hope I am not boring you."

"No. This is better than I expected." It was not good enough to just see a great piece of furniture or architecture because, beyond the aesthetic, she wanted to know what made a thing special. In order to have the best you must be able to identify it, and she told herself, one day everything she owned would be the best.

"I pass this house on the way to mass. I go to St. Monica's. I have wanted to see this place for a long time."

Ghost ended the tour where his mother would have begun, in the foyer, "These floors are limestone. It was pulled up out of the Trinity River. My family owns 1200 acres up there on 'The Island'".

Dubbed 'The Island' it is a ten-mile peninsula that is made from the Trinity River wrapping around on itself.

Ninety percent of the people that live on The Island were African American. That's where his family originated. No one but his grandfather's brother his Uncle Henry lived up there now.

"We go up there every summer," he added. "I didn't this summer, because of my mother."

When his mind ran across his mother, he dropped in mood and momentum.

"Where is your mother?"

"She passed. Right before school ended."

"Oh…I'm, I'm sorry."

"Me too."

He looked into Felicia's eyes. She was becoming sad. Her empathy lifted him in a way nothing since his mother's death had, and he smiled.

"I want to show you something."

He grabbed her hand and led her out through the front door and across the huge front lawn to the west corner of the gate. Tucked in the corner, nestled behind a curve of trees was a bench. It was his mother's favorite place outside, and Felicia could see why. The overhanging branches of the trees combined with the shrubbery made it nearly invisible, yet from that vantage point, they could see nearly the entire estate. The way the house set at an angle, they could see the front and part of the backyard. They could see Lil Eggy was chasing Pink around the pool. They could see Tanasha coming out of the pool house with Denny Ray. Tanasha twitched her nose and walked over to Keyanda. They exchanged words then looked up to Ghost's bedroom window. Keyanda shrugged her shoulder; their speculation was clear.

"What's the depth of you'll situations?" Felicia

asked.

"Who?"

"You and Keyanda," she asked.

"Me and Keyanda… Shallow…Ain't no situation."

Felicia laughed, "Well it's obvious she's feeling something."

"We hooked up once, but it wasn't nothing."

"Maybe to you, but she's feeling something."

"Normally, I don't put folks in other folks business, but from the angle of the conversation, you are flying into my private life."

Felicia expression showed her to pause.

"I didn't mean that to burn your wings. Trust me, that's the direction I want you to go." Felicia smiled.

"I said that to say I respect that what is done privately is meant to stay private. But what we about to do, this me and you, it is gone be epic, and for that, we got to be straight off the muscle."

'Off the muscle' she didn't know what that meant, but he seemed to be opening up, so she didn't interrupt.

"It was right after my mom died. I needed somebody. I probably shouldn't have slept with her, because I knew she was crushing on me, but I didn't lie to her. She knew what time it was just like she knows what time it is." Ghost went on, "That is one of the I ams, from the book of Benny Wu. I am too great for rape."

Wait she thought what did he say *The book of Benny Wu*? She had let it pass when he said that other thing, off the muscle, but this book of Benny Wu, he would have to explain.

"Is that your friend upstairs, the one sleeping in the guest room? He wrote a book of the bible? Is he a Mormon or something?" she questioned trying to get a grasp.

Ghost laughed, "Naw, not my partner…His daddy…well he wasn't any Mormon, he's a convict. Well, not anymore, he was executed. Well, wait, that's complicated.

"Sounds pretty clear to me."

He went on to explain about the book and how Benny Wu used it as a guide.

Felicia wondered what advice a convicted prisoner on death row could have.

Ghost tried to think of a way to clean it up and said, "I know this is going to come off raw but consider the source." By that he meant a convicted murderer trying to teach his son how to respect women, stay out of jail, and off of death row. "This is from the book of Benny Wu," Ghost took a breath and began reciting.

'If a woman wants to give you… some,
Whatever the recompense, it's hers to give;
If you take anything even with a lie its theft.
And theft of… sex is rape.'"

She was impressed that he lived to such a high moral code, whatever the source.

Ghost collapsed down beside her on the bench. He had just met her, but he wanted to trust her. He needed to confide in someone, *but secrets should be like teeth you should take them to the grave*, also from the book. So he talked around it.

"Have you ever did something wrong, but turns out it was the only way to make things right?"

"You mean like Judas?"

"What?"

"In the Bible, Judas, he betrayed Christ, but now

everybody can be saved."

Ghost, who did even know how they got on the subject of the Bible, was lost in the comparison, "So what are you saying?"

"I am saying that what Judas did, needed to be done. Somebody had to betray Christ. People don't like it. We make Judas out to be a villain. He sat right there beside Christ. Why didn't Jesus stop him? Because it was necessary! How were we to be saved if Christ wasn't crucified?"

"If you think about it Judas is just as responsible for salvation as Christ."

"I don't know if I would go that far."

Ghost stood up, and he left the weight of what he had done on that bench. He looked at his house and for the first time, realized it was his. It was left to him, but like his grandfather and his mother, he had to put skin in the game.

His chest swelled, and he felt more like a man than he had ever felt. He looked down at Felicia. She was more woman than he had ever known.

CHAPTER 6

"Before we pass judgment let us remember."

Benny Wu was raised by bears: barefoot, bare ass, and bare stomach. By sixteen, he was past tired. He was fed-up. He had all that he could take living like a roach off of scraps, handouts and hand me downs. No matter what Ghost said, to him, that's what it was, and he was sick of it. He was sick of being poor and everything that went with poverty. He was tired of trying to sleep hungry, in a hot dark house while his mother turned tricks on the other side of a too thin wall. Waking up to find out the only thing that has changed, with the coming of this new day, is now there is light. He was done with condemnations. Let he who has heard his mama gag for a rock, throw a rock. He clutched the thirty-two hundred dollars of the money that he got for the truck tight in his fist. He was through living like a vagabond.

Ghost was indebted to him. Their relationship had always been one-sided, but now for the first time, he had the power. And those other two, they did whatever Ghost said. Ghost never took advantage of that, but Benny Wu would. Aw yeah, he was about to use it to the fullest.

'Never let your right hand know what your left hand is doing' Benny Wu thought as he had his uncle drop him off on the corner, "Remember, don't turn your phone on until you are back at home."

He said goodbye and watched him drive off, and then walked two blocks, cut through the field and crossed the street. It was almost morning when he stood in front of the gate...

He walked through to the back where Ghost was sitting on the deck waiting on the sun. In late summer, it would rise over the front corner of the gate.

Lost in thought, Benny Wu was in striking distance of Ghost before he noticed him, but Ghost didn't jump. He turned slowly and smiled a bit. Benny Wu didn't know quite how to take that.

"I thought you would be a little more excited to see me," Benny Wu said.

"I knew there was nothing to worry about" Ghost replied.

"You mean you knew you couldn't get in trouble, once I left with-" Ghost cut him off by raising his finger to his lips. Benny Wu looked around.

"It's nothing," Ghost said as he led Benny Wu through the back yard to the front of the house, where he was sure even a sleepy ear could not hear.

"Who's here?"

"Denny Ray is laid-up with Tanasha in the pool house."

"Man this ain't no time for-"

Once again, Ghost stopped him, this time with a slight chuckle: He found it amusing how alike they were in thought. Different in manner, but alike in thought, "I told him, it was cool. I thought it was a good idea. I figured we could use the alibis. Anyway I told them you were in Chuck's room, asleep." Even though Benny nodded agreeing, Ghost left off the part about Felicia.

Benny digested the part about the girls and the alibi then said, "We are not done."

He laid out the rest of his plan. Well, the part Ghost needed to know. They would convince folks that the preacher just left. They had one great advantage.

"You have to speak to Pastor Walker this morning, before church tomorrow."

They looked back at the house and saw Denny Ray and Lil Eggy. They were just waking. Lil Eggy still had sleep in his eyes; he was rubbing them as they crossed the lawn. Denny was the first to speak, "So we good?"

"We're good!" Benny assured them.

"Where did you put it?" Lil Eggy said not quite satisfied, "The body," he added in a whisper.

"I am not going to tell you," Benny Wu said to all of them adding, "and after this we will never speak about it again."

"Why?" Lil Eggy seemed disappointed.

"You can't tell what you don't know, and the world will never know if we don't tell. They may speculate," Benny looked at each of them deeply, "but they will never know. After we leave here, on this, we have no comment. We never speak about this again."

Lil Eggy had to get it off his chest, "Well if I don't get to say this again that was bad ass shit."

"Naw Eggy that was necessary, and watch your mouth."

Ghost used to blame his disdain for profanity on his mother. She would say that profanity was the sign of an uneducated mind trying to express itself, but she had passed, and he still demanded it.

Benny Wu had thought about what he wanted to say all night, "Wait. We are losing focus, or we are focused on the wrong thing... Ok, maybe he could have used some different words, but Lil Eggy was right. You are looking at four of the baddest; I am sorry Ghost, motherfuckers in Acres Homes. Maybe all of Texas! Look at what just happened, we needed each other and look how we came through for each other.

"Especially you Denny... I'm the proudest of you... 'cause you weren't with it. But when it was time... you didn't break ground; you dug your heels in. You bucked up. And Lil Eggy 'whoa true soldier for real, the young dawua for real. Like we were last night, I want us always to be like that, for each other. You'll are like my brothers; I'd go to war for you."

"What are you saying?" Ghost said.

"I'm saying I would die for you; would you die for me?"

"You know I would," Ghost said then the others fired their yeses off.

"If we will crawl into the pit of hell for each other why won't we climb out together with each other?"

Benny explained that he wanted to form a set, a gang. They were already bound to each other in an inseparable way. They had proven themselves to each other as well as themselves. Now it was time to take it to the world.

Ghost interrupted, "Benny Wu I appreciate all that

49

Y'all have done, but I made a mistake."

"And we had your back…'and did what was necessary…That's what I am saying man; this is necessary. Money is necessary … School is about to start, and every last one of us is wearing something of yours… Lil Eggy this is his last year at MC. He needs those ugly uniforms, shoes, and shit, and this is our senior year. I don't mean any disrespect, but Ms. Brenda Fay is gone. What are you going to do?"

"I have the insurance money."

"How long is that gone last with the bills around this big house, taxes and all the other stuff? Ghost, what about when it's gone? That's what I am talking about. That's why you have to talk to Pastor Walker this morning. I got the whole thing figured out. Look Ghost; we are in the same boat now." He looked around at the massive estate perfectly manicured, Brenda Fay's 735 that Barry had been driving and said, "Ok, maybe it ain't the same boat."

They all laughed a little and then Benny Wu got back serious, "but Bruh you sinking too. It might be a little slower, but you're taking on water. Why sit here and watch your beautiful boat fill up and sink, we can patch up together, and get somewhere."

He looked at Denny Ray. Regardless of what he had said he knew Denny felt like he punked out. So Benny Wu put him on the spot, "Denny Ray, Bruh, are you with me?"

Denny Ray stuck his hand out, and then he began to feel something. Fear, regret, maybe a little corny, he was about to pull it back when Benny Wu grabbed his wrist, and looked him in the eyes and said, "I got you, through whatever, from now to whenever, whatever comes next, I'm scrapping with you!"

Instinctively, Lil Eggy grabbed Benny Wu's wrist, and they looked at Ghost. Who joined in just as Benny Wu knew he would, but how could he not?

As uneasy as he was somewhere in his gut he knew Benny Wu was right. There was some truth in what he said. There are things in this world that are necessary. He didn't want to be the villain, no matter the necessity. He thought about Felicia and wondered if she could love a Judas.

"If we gonna have a set we gotta have a name," Lil Eggy added.

Benny thought things like that were juvenile and not necessary, and was about to say so when Ghost said, "Disciples of Judas…The Necessary Evil."

For the first time in a long time, Benny Wu smiled for real. To run a group so bent on having cash, they would cross the Lord. It was perfect.

Benny Wu did not see the curtain move as they walked back to the house. He was told that Pink had crashed somewhere, but when he found her lying in his bed, perspicacity is the only way to explain it.

The curtain was slightly cracked. He remembered Brenda Fay had bought the darkest curtains that she could find because the sun came up straight through those upstairs windows and spilled through the entire house. Before electricity, it would have been considered engineering genius; however, since its inception and the creation of the double shift, it was an annoyance. Benny Wu had left the curtains overlapping.

Pink was lying on one side of the bed, but the other side was rumpled as well. The space in the middle was smooth. He knew she had not rolled to the other side. She had gotten up. She had her back to him, but her face was placed on the pillow so that he could see her profile. He could tell from her eyes and the depth of her breathing, all he needed to know. She had been at the window. She had seen them in the front of the house, and she knew that he was not there last night. Now she has the nerve to be laying there pretending to be sleep.

Pink had heard him enter the room but did not hear him cross. He was so quiet and then finally, she heard something. The nightstand, it slid open and then closed. She felt anxious and excited. Why wasn't he saying anything? What was he doing? What had he taken out of the nightstand or put in?

She could feel him, standing beside the bed, watching her. He was quiet, why wasn't he saying anything she thought.

She wondered if he was taking his clothes off. What if he was? What if he got in the bed? What would she do? The thought of him standing there semi-nude, his hard chiseled body crawling beside her, on top of her, it was more than her little radiator could handle. She could feel her temperature rising, her body slightly perspiring and moisten. She began to overheat. Her legs were on fire. She wanted to readjust but was afraid to move. Just as she was about to fake wake, he said, "You can stop acting like you're asleep."

Benny Wu had spoken so soft, had she been asleep, his words would not have disturbed her, but she wasn't.

He had never noticed it before, but Pink was pretty. That part didn't matter much, he had to do what he had to do, but she was cute.

Benny Wu would never trust Pink to lie for him.

Lying is too complicated to trust to someone on drugs. He was in an awkward position because she could blow his alibi.

She opened her eyes, and he was standing over her. He was not naked as she had both feared and hoped, but he was as delicious as she was hungry. He squatted beside the bed his face was two inches from her nose, "Let's be grown."

"Aw," Pink replied.

" You came in here last night, looking for me. You were full of them bars …fell asleep. You did even know I was sleeping in that chair, but that's not important."

Actually, it was. He had to plant the seed that he was there. Then he moved her to a completely different part of the garden.

"You came in here to give it to me. You were going to blame it on the Xanax, but that is what was up."

Pink was flabbergasted, how could he know that? She did want him, and she did come in there looking for him; she thought she had looked over there.

"On the cool, Pink, I would let it go at that. But this morning you woke up, looked out that window sober, saw me and got back in my bed."

"Ah," she started to speak.

"Ah," He cut her off, "let's not lie. You and I have a perfect record. I have never lied to you. You have never lied to me. Let's keep it a 100. And for the record, ain't nothing wrong with you diggin' me. Now, I think…I think, you been lying there, thinking that I was about to climb in that bed, twist you up and bang you sideways."

She didn't know what to think, so she bent her face like she was slightly shocked. The only thing that was shocking is how accurate he was.

"Don't worry, that is exactly what I had in mind, but if I am wrong, you're awake now, you can get up, gone go downstairs, No harm no foul."

Pink didn't know what to think. It was like he was in her head. She did come into that room looking for him. She thought that the room was empty, but she was high; obviously, he had been there she thought. He was for sure here now. He was as real as the decision that she had to make. Was she going to get up and act like he had her mistaken, or would she take her chance? She did want Benny Wu, but he had called her out. He made her sound like she was just a hot little whore. How could she have him, and save face?

She did the only thing she could. She jumped up off the bed like she was offended, stormed across the room like she was leaving. She figured she would surprise him. Instead of bolting out of the door, she would lock it. In that moment of indecision, in that tiny tick of time, when he believed that she was leaving, she would salvage a scrap of her dignity. But when she turned, he had already taken his shirt off and was tearing open the condom that he got out of the nightstand when he entered the room.

CHAPTER 7

"This ain't no practice run."

Ghost would tell Pastor Walker the same thing that he would tell the police if it came to that, but if he did it right. On Sunday they would announce in church that Barry had moved on. Barry didn't have many friends, so a general announcement should satisfy anyone looking for him. If he did it wrong, Pastor Walker was also the Houston Police Chaplin, and he would for sure call the police.

Benny Wu coached him, giving him the fundamentals of telling a good lie, straight from the book.

Practice your lie. Not the words. If you practice what you're going to say, it may sound staged. Instead, re-write what happen in your mind. Go over what happened again and again, until you can see it happening. Then when you do speak, be vague in your account as well as in your responses. Remember telling a good lie is in the detail, but too much is just as bad as not enough.

Tell an independent lie. A lie should stand alone, on its own, like a table. It should not involve anyone else. That way, no one can muck it up. Keep it simple, using as much of the truth as possible, because no matter how well

crafted, a lie stinks.

Benny Wu concluded, "But most important, don't forget Pastor Walker ain't no fool. Not by a long shot."

If Benny Wu ever spoke the truth, he spoke it then. Pastor Walker graduated from Dartmouth, but he dusted off his common sense just as often as he did the diploma on the wall behind his desk. Even more formidable, like the old folks would say, "he was saved and filled with the Holy Ghost." Truly, each of his steps was metered by his love for God, and the fear that he might show himself unworthy. He had been their pastor, Ghost and his mother's since she got saved. When she found God, the Bible was her map; but Pastor Walker for sure was her guide.

Normally, on Saturdays, he would not be disturbed. In preparation for Sunday service, he spent all day in meditation and would not take calls. However, an urgent message from Brenda Fay's son compelled him to make an exception. Brenda Fay was a devoted member and long-time friend, and her death had vexed him much.

Ghost relaxed when his wife said to hold on he was coming to the phone. That was much better. Ghost had feared that she would tell him to come by. No matter how prepared a person, it is harder for a person of conscience to lie to someone's face. But over the phone, a person can be whomever they want to be. Over the phone, they can confidently just let their lie go. They don't have to look a person in the eyes, measuring the disbelief in their glance, or the mistrust in their leer. Yes, the best place for a lie to be told, at least for the liar is over the phone.

"Marcus, my wife said that you had a problem."

"Yes, Sir."

"Well, don't worry, son. I will be there within

twenty minutes."

"Wha-wha-what?"

"Yeah, son don't you worry. Whatever it is that has troubled you enough to call me, after all, you've been through, you don't worry son; I'm on my way."

Men of God seldom think about anything. That is because they pray on everything. Pastor Walker was not an exception; he was the rule. His every thought was elevated with "thus saith the LORD," and he had been in prayer ever since he hung up the phone.

When he drove up to the gate, his spirit was uneasy. Ghost buzzed him in and was standing outside by the time the pastor drove up.

"I wanted to speak to you outside because I didn't tell any of my friends what happen," Ghost muttered.

That was number one, don't involve anyone in your lie. He went on to explain that his stepfather had been watching him. He told his pastor about the holes and computer.

"Son, you didn't tell anyone? Not even Peggy's boy, your friend...aw...what's his name?"

Pastor Walker calling Benny Wu's mother by her first name knocked Ghost for a loop; Benny Wu had never been to church. Ghost didn't think Pastor Walker knew him, but he just called his mother by her first name. That took him a little off his game. If Pastor Walker knew them that well, would he believe Ghost didn't tell Benny Wu?

"Benny Wu." Ghost replied.

"Yeah, Benny Wu, you didn't say anything to him?"

If he said yes, Benny Wu would have to lie to support his lie, and his lie must stand alone.

"No! I didn't tell him especially."

The greatest aid to a lie is the person being lied to. If they have any desire to believe, like faith, all they need is the size of a mustard seed, and they can believe. They will find a way to believe.

Acres Homes is like a small-town everybody knows everybody. Pastor Walker knew Brenda Fay and her struggles. He could understand a son not wanting to pile shame on her grave. And from what he had heard of Benny Wu, keeping him in the dark in a matter like this he perceived as probably prudent, but he wanted to believe.

Ghost took him into the house to show him the holes in the walls. At the front door, the pastor began to take off his shoes. It was Brenda Fay's custom. Ghost had fallen out of the practice, but he kicked his slippers into the corner, and they shuffled upstairs. He showed him the holes in the wall.

"My God son, how long has this been going on?"

"He always made me feel, you know creepy, but the holes and stuff a little after Mama died."

He could hear Benny Wu saying mix in as much truth as possible and continued, "Three maybe four nights before last night, I reached my limit."

"He didn't touch you did he?"

The Pastor did it again. Each time he asked a question; it would take Ghost quickly off his guard. It wasn't the complexity of the questions; there wasn't any trickery or deception there. Ghost was confounded by his compassion. It was overwhelming; to the point Ghost found himself telling the truth.

"It felt like he was, I mean it didn't bother me at first. Then the other day, I was with a friend of mine." Ghost hadn't thought when he began to tell the story to his pastor that he was having sex in it, but he was telling the truth, so he told the truth.

"We were…" he looked at Pastor Walker knowing clearly well what he would call it and said, "fornicating."

The pastor's look was neither approving nor disapproving as he nodded for him to go on. Ghost would not stop until he was done.

"Normally, I would never have company when he was home. Because I… you know but I told her about the holes. We laughed about it, called him a horny old man. You know. It was funny. I talked her into it, I said, 'If the old freak wants to peep, we should give him something to see.' So we did. It was cool at first and then my friend, she got really into it. We had been under the cover. You know discreet with it, really more messing with him than with each other. I could already hear him in the closet going crazy. Before I knew it, I was on my back; she came from under the covers turns her backside to the hole and started touching herself… doing … You know… me. Well, he really started going crazy. I could hear him in the closet kicking like a pack of rats in a sack. It was supposed to be funny, but I finished, and I guess he finished too because he stopped kicking… It got quiet… all I could think about was him. I kept seeing him in my mind. All I could think about was him. Laying in there all sweaty, sticky and smiling. It made me feel sweaty and sticky too…but nasty. I couldn't get his sweaty, sticky face out of my mind….and my friend… She was smiling like she really did something, but it felt like she was just a glove on his hand. Her mouth was his mouth. I was sick, and her smile was making me sicker."

We walked past each other for a couple of days, me

and Barry. Not really saying anything. Then the day before yesterday when he was going to work he smiled at me; he looked just like I imagined he did in that closet. It made me sick. Just like that night. I thought about it all day. By the time he came home, I had worked it out. He did the same thing he did every day walk through the back door and tossed his keys on the table. This time when he did, I picked them up and left the keys to the truck where they were.

While he was in the shower, I took his computer. He has porn all over it. He would flip the screen around trying to get me to watch. One time in the kitchen he showed me a clip of two guys... He tried to play it off like it popped up by accident. Anyway, I took it. I got in my Mama's car and called him from the gate... I told him if he didn't leave I was going to the police and give them his computer and tell them what he did."

"Lord Jesus, son what did he say?"

"He started apologizing; promising to leave and never come back, begging me not to go to the police. I could hear him throwing his stuff together as he was begging. I hung up the phone and went to pick up Benny Wu, and when I got back, he was gone."

And it was done. The lie was told. Ghost wondered if he believed him. It was hard to tell because Ghost's head was down, and he could not see Pastor Walker's eyes. Just as he was about to raise his head to know, Pastor Walker's feet walked into his field of view as the pastor hugged him.

"I am so sorry son."

He believed.

Ghost took a breath, a short sigh of relief. However, having Pastor Walker to believe him was just the windup; the pitch is the important part. He could not be too direct. If he just came out and said 'now if you could just tell that to the congregation, I would appreciate' it wouldn't sit well. He could not come right out and ask him to do his dirty work. He would do as Benny Wu instructed lay the seed and let it grow into what he needed.

He looked Pastor Walker in the eyes, "I'm okay. I don't think he is ever coming back here. I am only worried about this house. This is my mother's house no matter what happens. I will never lose it."

The reason some people get caught in a lie is not because of the way they tell, the lie, but it is the way they told the truth. The pastor like God loved the truth. What the boy said moved something in his spirit and he had a strong feeling that was the truest thing that he heard all day. Swirled in the young man's truth was something, but that didn't make a difference either. His responsibility was the same. Pastor Walker pulled out his phone to call the police.

"Wait a minute," Ghost said as he grabbed his phone, "I don't want to go to the police."

"I have to," the pastor said as he reclaimed his phone and began to dial, "Son, it is against the law to know a child has been abused and not reported. We must render unto Cesar that which is Cesar's."

CHAPTER 8

"Sweetly deceptive, woman is the hunter posing as prey."

There were cops everywhere. At least that is how Ghost felt, actually there were only three. Two technicians and the detective had just arrived and were standing in the front of the house talking to Pastor Walker, but Ghost felt like there were cops all over the place.

Finally, Benny Wu answered. Ghost had been trying to call him since Pastor Walker walked downstairs to wait for the police. Now they were gathering in front of the house, about to come in.

He whispered excitedly, "Where have you been?"

"I was asleep."

"Benny it's laws everywhere. Pastor Walker called the police!"

"I figured he might do that."

"What?" Ghost almost choked in disbelief.

"I figured he would probably call the police."

"WHAT THE HELL BENNIE! With all this figuring you are doing, you didn't figure to tell ME! How did you figure this is a good idea?"

"Cause it don't make no difference," he chuckled, "They

are looking for him you are on this phone acting like their looking for you. Now you know the rule on this."

He meant talking on the phone. Benny Wu, like many geniuses, lived on the edge of a state of paranoia. The knowledge of what could be done, constantly clashing against what is being done. Benny believed that "someone" was listening to everything said on or around a telephone. "Gf (government-friendly) Ghost … You got this …Be bout business, and I will be there as soon as they are gone."

Felicia was wonderstruck. She had hardly slept all night, excited about her prospects but then what young woman wouldn't be. Marcus was a great catch. He was cute, he was smart, and he was paid. Not to mention that house, that fabulous, fabulous house. All morning, she fantasized about that house, being in it. Cooking, cleaning, having company and throwing parties. On her list to be a happy, fulfilled woman, there were only five things. And if things worked out between her and Ghost, that was three of them down.

'You need to call before you come by!' There were some accommodating dummies, but Felicia wasn't one. You can't tell a bee where to buzz, especially the queen.

Ghost had said that he was not involved with anyone. If that was or wasn't the truth, she felt it wasn't just a woman's right to be informed; it was her responsibility. And she wanted to see him, to see if it had all been a dream. Things always look different in the daylight; that's why she waited for a decent hour before dropping by unexpectedly.

You can tell a lot about a man by dropping in on him. Does he get upset, become agitated and irate or does he flash all 32 teeth and reach for you so fast that he lifts you off your feet, the momentum of his joy sending you swinging and giggling like a school girl?

There is also the chance that you could pop up on someone and find out that they already have someone. But it's best to know if you are dealing with a liar from the beginning.

Ghost recanted his story for the police. This time it was easier. The Belvedere calmed his nerves and knowing a mistake meant spending the rest of his very short life in prison, strengthened his resolve.

The investigator was beautiful. Her hair was pulled back into a ponytail, and she wore a pants suit trying to dial back her sexy, but it wasn't working. The polyester pants hugged her hips showcasing a quite impressive figure. At first, Ghost felt a little odd speaking with her about such intimate affairs, but that was eased by her demeanor. Even her sympathy fell on professional lines, "I am sorry you have to go through this again. Could you show me the holes?"

They went up the stairs to the room. Ghost had not been in the room much since his mother passed. With Barry, being such a pervert, he was afraid of what he may find. Even when Barry's things were discarded Benny Wu sent Ghost out, he said it was so that Ghost wouldn't know what happened. That way if ever asked he would not have to lie.

"Let's get this," she barked to one of the techs. He pulled out a small camera and began to record as she took a pen and pointed to each of the holes.

There were four in all. They were all in line about two maybe three inches above the floor.

"There is only one on the other side of the wall," Ghost pointed out.

She knew that the various holes gave the suspect a range of vantages into the child's room but what she said was, "We will look at it in a moment."

Sexual assault is not like other crimes. It is as much, if not more, of an assault on the mind. With a physical assault, the bruising is clear, but with an assault on the psyche, there is a reoccurring ambush, which sends some peeping around corners for the rest of their lives. The detective's intent was to protect him, "We have it from here. Reverend Walker, you'll can go downstairs and wait for us there." Ghost could hear that professional sympathy.

"No," Ghost exclaimed emphatically, "this is my house. I am good, but thank you."

She pulled out a small ultra-violet light in the shape of a pen and shined it into the closet. She started at the first holes and scanned slowly out. They didn't see anything initially but then about three feet down, they saw it.

"Boo yaw! Perv juice," the young tech yelped. The inspector gave him a disapproving leer and then glanced back at Ghost.

It was difficult to say how he felt. The expression on his face was just shy of mortified. The wall, as well as the floor, was splattered with ejaculates.

Detective DeValo looked at the young man and sympathized, but that was a problem for another professional. Her job was to investigate this child abuse and stop this predator.

"You two," she said speaking to the two technicians,

"collect samples from the carpet. I need to get very clear pics."

The young tech got excited at his chance to search for evidence. She checked his enthusiasm, "Let me know the moment you find anything."

Both technicians nodded and immediately went to work. She looked at Ghost, "You come with me."

They walked downstairs, "You said that you had his computer."

"Yes Ma' am…"

She cut him off, "and I am going to need the name of the girl… I have to speak to the girl."

"No."

"Excuse me?" Detective DeValo was taken aback by his blatant defiance.

"I said NO," fortified by the liquor he spoke with extreme confidence.

"I wasn't asking."

He looked at Pastor Walker, "We are going to have to keep her out of this."

"That young lady was also assaulted, she may need-"

Ghost turned and cut his pastor off saying, "Well then forget it." He was standing at the foot of the curved staircase his words had stopped both of them coming down. The amber step they shared was so wide the pastor, and the detective stood three feet apart as Ghost pointed between them both adding, "If either of you tries to put her in this I won't cooperate. I'll take it back. Say I was lying, but I am not doing her like that."

He walked off. While she was impressed by Ghost's gallantry, it created an impasse. There were obvious signs of abuse, but there wasn't anything that could be called evidence. Gross as all of this was, it could be explained away. She knew without his testimony; she could not go any further. She took off after him saying, "Okay, we will keep her out of it for now."

"No, either we do this without her, or I am out," Ghost had her up against the wall.

"Just get me the computer." The computer was important. Beyond the possibility that he had used a camera and had recorded the event, there was the more assured guarantee that she would find child porn.

They looked at each other Ghost's resolve was set.

"Okay, I will do everything I can."

"Everything!"

"Everything."

Now Felicia was not completely uncouth. Her intent was to call while on the way, makeup any excuse to see him. Something so good he could not pass it up. Then swing in before he had a chance to clean up. She picked out the perfect story and the skirt to match. It was a cute little Guess skirt she really should have thrown away last summer. Of course, she would never really wear it anywhere, but she would not tell him that. What she would tell him was she, and her grandmother had argued about it being too short.

She would say something about a picnic then throw in an 'I wanted to know what you think?' and watch him scramble. She smiled and pressed dial, and her mind began to run through different scenarios. 'You say it's too short,' 'let you be the judge,' 'I can get what out of my mind' 'oh I see all picnics are we from now on'. She smiled to herself, as the line picked up. To her surprise, it was a woman,

"Your balance is insufficient to make this call."

"What?" She said out loud. She was confused she had just paid her bill two days before, and it wasn't due until the first. She needed to pull over, call customer service and get this straight. She was going to stop at the corner store by his house, but she saw Pink and who she thought looked like Keyanda, going in. It is strange how you never notice a person before, and then after you all meet, you start seeing them everywhere. Whatever the situation was with that, she did not want to see them.

So she kept going. She was in this little piece of a skirt, her phone wasn't working, and the last thing she wanted was to see them. What she needed was a place to pull over get her receipt and then call T-Mobile.

It seemed like she had just turned the corner but was in front of his gate. It was open, so she pulled in. Inherently, there is a problem with being self-absorbed with all of one's attention centrally focused; some things get missed. Like she did not notice the other cars in the drive as she drove passed them, nor did she notice Ghost, Detective DeValo and Pastor Walker walking out of the front door. Like a pigeon, she flew to the place where she parked last night.

Ghost was a little lit. He struck out to the car as soon as he saw it and was at her window before she put it in park. Although he never had before, he leaned in and kissed her on the cheek. It was quick and natural, but with her being so engrossed, she hardly noticed. He looked in her twisted face and said, "What's wrong?"

"It's my phone."

Pastor Walker and Detective DeValo walked up. Detective DeValo discreetly wrote down the license plate, but it was the pastor who spoke first, "Marcus aren't you going to introduce us to your friend?"

"Oh, Pastor Walker," he had forgotten just that fast they were there.

"Pastor?" Felicia yelped looking down at her skirt.

Ghost grabbed the door handle and opened it. She pulled it back. She gestured with her head pointing downwards with her eyes to her skirt and had he been sober he may have noticed, but he wasn't and didn't. He pulled the door open again this time almost snatching her out of the car. From a combination of awe, wonder and confusion Ghost's tongue nearly fell from his mouth as he helped her from the car to her feet.

When Pastor Walker was a young man, he asked an older preacher, "How do you keep from stumbling?" The preacher told him "Preaching is a lot like driving as long as you look through the windows and you keep your eyes on the road, you will do fine." He looked the young lady in her eyes and said, "I am Pastor Walker."

"Pastor," She said to Ghost trying to hide behind the door. She took his hand, and for the first time she was ashamed to say her name, but she did, "I am Felicia Gilmore."

"I am sorry I didn't mean to drop in like this, I just wanted to ask you if this skirt was too short."

"Yes!" they all said in unison.
She looked at Ghost embarrassed, "I am so sorry. I was going to call but my phone."

However, Ghost missed her apology. His eyes were fixed on the detective. He knew the detective would assume Felica was the young lady in question. And he was right but Detective DeValo was true to her word and without even introducing herself made her exit, "We have all we need here. Ms. Gilmore, it was nice to meet you." She turned to walk away and then quickly turned back. Ghost's anxiety did the same cha-cha. He was relieved when she didn't say anything before, but there was her face smack in the center of the scene again. Somewhere between, what do you want and please move the hell on, Ghost smiled at Detective DeValo like he was constipated.

Detective DeValo leaned in and said to the girl, "If you have to ask, treat it like it is! I used that with everything pertaining to being a woman," then she walked away without a second glance.

Felicia was so embarrassed. She made her way into the house to try to find something to put on. She wanted to go to the T-Mobile store before she went home.

She was upstairs, so she didn't see Benny Wu. Careful not to be seen, he was true to his word and came out of the trail, just as the police were leaving.

"Dude, what's up?" Benny Wu chimed.

"It's just like you said, Bennie. They are looking for a perv!"

"They ain't going to never find." Benny Wu pulls him over by the car. It was a 735 BMW, his mother's pride and joy. It was steel gray with matching leather interior. She had gotten it a few months before she passed. The insurance paid it off as well.

"Wait, whose car is that?" he pointed to the pink Honda Accord in the drive.

"Nothing, it's this new girl I met, Tanasha's cousin."

"Cool, then you can use her car; I am taking this one."

Most people would have an objection to someone pulling off in their 735, but Ghost didn't blink. Benny Wu pulled out the money he got for the truck and gave Ghost 3200 of it, "Here take this money. You take care of the school clothes don't worry about me. I am going to get mine on the road."

"What's up Bennie?"

Benny Wu started laying out his plan to go and get the rest of the money.

"Money! What money?"

"When your mama died, the insurance was divided in half. I'm fina get the rest of that money."

"Benny that's in the bank, you can't get that money man. We need to leave that alone."

"I have all of his information. I am that Man, Man. I used his ATM all through Louisiana."

"How did you get his pin?"

"Come on dude. Yours 6297, your mama's was 2393, old man Putts 4545, I remember the number of anybody that uses their card around me. I can't help it. But this idiot had it wrote down on a card in his wallet. It's your address. The moron never had a bank account until he met your mama. He didn't deserve that money."

"And you do!"

Benny Wu was shocked and amazed; Ghost had never stood up to him before. Not like that, not about something like this. He didn't know it was the liquor talking and almost came at it differently.

"Whether or not we deserve it, I'm going to get it!"

Ghost was like his younger brother, and he was just going to have to listen, "Take that money and get Li Eggy's and Denny Ray's gear for school. Whatever you do, don't put any money in their hands. Idiots will come back here with four pairs of shoes."

They laughed and then Benny Wu said, "I promise I got this. Oh, and Lil Eggy, make sure you get his uniforms and some hard bottoms. I am getting a pair myself."

"What?"

"Hard bottoms, this is going to be a different type of year."

Ghost felt sure of that; there was no doubt. He had buried his mother, murdered his step-father and was beginning to feel that to conceal it, he had signed a deal with the devil. He wrestled with his appreciation but smiled at his friend as he drove off.

CHAPTER 9

"Sometimes you just get lucky."

They say that ignorance is bliss; this is one of the few times that they were right. Ghost was as happy as a hobo on a ham sandwich. He and his beautiful new girlfriend, laughing through the mall, ballin' store after store, all the time facilitating that gaiety was ignorance. All those things he didn't know. For example, he did not know that had he not given the computer to Detective DeValo this whole thing would be over, but he didn't know. Just like he didn't know Detective DeValo had been born with the worst of curses. She was born beautiful in a dysfunctional family. How could he know that she was raped and abused as a child? That for her child abuse was not a game of most convictions. She was dogmatic about finding and stopping all abusers.

There were so many things that he didn't know. Like he didn't know the men's public restroom, the one down the hall and across the room from Detective DeValo's desk, from time to time carried a scent. And that scent, every now and then, would crawl from under the door. Waft down that very long hallway and across that large room to find her nose. How would anyone know that the smell of urine would make her flashback in her pain? Back to being a little girl whose bladder was too small to stand the weight of a grown man pressing on it, making her go on herself. Back to being so ashamed and disgusted, that she would leave it. Praying that the stench would get so bad no one would ever want her. How could he know? Even she didn't know, but every time that smell hit her nose, it was like pulling the chain of a pit-bull.

Detective DeValo sat there looking at the computer screen in a jaw-tight snarl. She had run the images on the hard drive through the database of known illegal images and got twenty-seven hits. She had followed the links and found that most of them came from reputable, sites if there is such a thing. They were pictures that have been floating around the Internet for so long it was impossible to place the origin. While they can get you in a lot of trouble, a lawyer worth, his salt could get you off, but it was enough to establish probable cause to get a warrant.

Detective DeValo refused to pack a purse. She felt it was feminizing. She hit send grabbed her keys and headed to her soror, District Attorney Nora Radcliff. First, she would get a warrant. Then she could turn on the heat, freeze his assets and drag him out of hiding. She had already been tracking him by ATM. He was moving all through Louisiana. She thought to try to find a job and a place to hunker down.

What was actually happening was Benny Wu was driving through the countryside, from town to town, looking for something specific with nothing in particular, in mind. He had been searching for days, withdrawing the card's limit daily. He made his withdrawals from gas stations, older convenience stores and other places like that with no cameras. All the time casing banks from eight to six every day like a job; he went from bank to bank. There were only twenty-four branches, and they were spread all across the state. He logged where he had been and where he had yet to go carefully on the map, making sure not to overlap or miss.

What he was looking for sounded simple; a manager's car, no more than four years old with a dent. His thinking was the banking industry hinges on people paying their bills, the leveling of credit and the assessment of interest. Bankers pay their bills. They watch each other pay their bills and keep records. The only way a person would get into an accident and not fix it is they can't afford it or better; the insurance paid them, and the money went to someplace else. Eight to one, Benny Wu was convinced that type of irresponsibility would signal an addict. That is what he was looking for, a dope fiend, but he would settle for a gambler or trick, anyone desperate. He had lived with a crackhead, so he could spot desperation. Crackheads are notoriously desperate people. He learned to notice that fidgety undertone that comes from constantly searching for an answer, that sweaty panic of a feverish need. Like fear, desperation is so powerful it is pungent, and to Benny Wu, its oily musk was an aphrodisiac.

There had been a few times he was close, but they never panned out. There was a Malibu in Jena, then a Bronco in Jonesboro, but both turned out to be nothing.

Then in Vicksburg, he thought he had found it, but when he saw the guy coming out of the bank, he knew he was wrong. It was a black guy in his middle ages. His tousled messiness came from a general lack of care.

But then just as it always seems, when he was about

to give up, he saw it, in Winnsboro. A gray Magnum, it was clean all except for the front left fender. He was so excited he parked immediately and jumped out. He went up to the car it was better than he could have hoped. The front tip of the hood was slightly bent as well and in the dent, trickled like gold, a beautiful vain of rust. It was as an old dent.

He was so excited. He would not try to hit another bank, this was it, and he knew it. Instead, he took the time to get himself together. If he was right, he was going now. He didn't like to work on an empty stomach, so he went to get something to eat. There wasn't very much in the little town he trusted, but he was in Louisiana, there was a Popeye's down the street. He bought a three piece with red beans and rice and drove back. He parked at the gas station across the street, to eat and wait for the bank to close.

He wanted to call Ghost, to tell him he thought he had finally found his fish, but he was afraid Felicia would answer. He didn't know why Ghost would let her answer the burner phone, nor did he understand why it bothered him. But it did.

He tried to talk to Ghost about it. He said they were too deep for that, implying that she may overhear something that would cause a problem. He knew coming out of his mouth that was a lie. In order for that to happen, he would have to slip and say something wrong. That would never happen. He had lied, and that lie bothered him even more. He and Ghost never lied to each other, and worse he didn't know why he had done it. He didn't know Felicia, had never even seen the girl, but something about her bothered him. However, rather than alienate his friend, he didn't bring it up again and, out of respect he tried to hide his disdain.

The last time he called, Ghost picked up, but as soon

as she heard Ghost call Benny Wu's name, her mood instantly changed. It was subtle, quiet even, only absent the tremble of a soft giggle. So faint that Ghost, who was in the same room with her didn't even notice but Benny did. Over those cheap burner phones, some 1200 miles away, driving through the backwoods of Louisiana, Benny heard it. It was like there was a beautiful little bell softly ringing and an elephant's big husky foot in one hateful step smashed it out. He turned his attention back to the bank. Something wasn't right.

Usually banks, like most places that deal with large amounts of cash, all the people leave at the same time. It is safer. Employees don't get caught alone, or left alone, but the bank manager didn't come out with everyone else. Everyone came out of the building got into their cars and pulled off, but the Dodge Magnum didn't move. That was strange enough, but no one came out of the building. He waited and waited, but the guy never came out. Maybe it was because it was the country. Country folks have a relaxed attitude he reasoned... Maybe he is working a little late... Maybe with the police station right down the street in plain sight, maybe they feel a little more comfortable out here ... Maybe ...

Maybe the guy's car was broke. Maybe he didn't even work at the bank. Maybe they're just letting him park there until he can get it towed. Maybe I made a mistake.

He was about to crank up and leave when the door to the bank cracked. He froze in his seat, but it was a woman who walked out. That wasn't right he thought. The car was beefy. It had 20" Akuza's rims and Pirelli tires on it; with the fat face grill, no girl puts a car together like that! He continued his thought summarizing if he had been wrong about that, maybe he was wrong about the whole thing. His plan was to follow the guy, understanding most men get off work and go straight to their vice. He was trying to figure out what to do. When she did the one thing, he never contemplated she would do. She drove straight to him.

Well, she drove up to the gas station. She jumped from the car a disheveled, nervous wreck, and bolted into the store so fast he didn't have a chance to get out, and was coming out before he had even gotten his self together. She was moving so fast that it forced him to come up from behind her, "Excuse me miss."

"Oh Lord Jesus!" she shouted, grabbing her chest. The middle-aged white woman was as country as buttermilk but, as they say in them parts, 'she was as fine as the hair on a frog's ass.'"

He threw his hands up to show her that there was nothing in them.

"I didn't mean to frighten you."

However, that is exactly what he did. She was scared. Not kind of scared but heart-pounding fear chokingly scared. Physically a knot rose in her throat, and she could not breathe. Even as she caught her breath, she could still fill the lump. Her mind raced as her eyes were flittering and scanning the parking lot.

Benny Wu could not figure out what she was looking for but said, "There is no one with me."

For the first time, she looked into his face, his handsomely chiseled face. She could tell he was too young to be the police, and he was black, so he wasn't one of them. That allowed her to relax a little. Benny Wu didn't know who she was looking for, but he knew that smell. It was the deliciously funky scent of desperation.

For Felicia it was exhilarating but, everybody loves shopping. Ghost was letting her handle it all. He liked surrendering the responsibility. Besides she was good at it. Anyone can just walk into a store and spend a bunch of money but, she knew how to shop. Where to get the real deals, plus she worked part-time at Marline's, it was a retail shop on 19th in the Heights. They boasted selling high-end stuff on consignment, but most of their things came from the wholesale thrift on Little York. A lot of the resale stores get their clothes from the Dollar Seventy-five.

When houses are foreclosed and, or they are abandoned, or when a store is going under, whatever the situation, the Dollar Seventy-five buys clothes in bulk by the pound. Then Tuesday night they close early and by Wednesday have it all on the racks for a $1.75 each. It's like black Friday every Wednesday morning. While there are some Moms and Pops in there looking for a deal, most are Mom and Pop shops struggling to pay their bills.

However, Felicia would not have to go through that. She worked for Ms. Marline, who had a special relationship with the owner, Ms. Rosalina. Ms. Rosalina worked for Ms. Marline long years ago. Ms. Rosalina didn't have a flair for fashion or sales, but she worked hard and was honest. So when the opportunity opened up, Ms. Marline helped her start her business. Long story short, Ms. Marline's store got first pick. Her buyers come in on Tuesday night while the store is closed and being stocked. This Tuesday Felicia was there with Ghost.

Shelia told Benny Wu all he needed to know. She was the manager of the bank, and if he could help her, she would bring the money to him.

"What are you going to do?"

Benny didn't read the Bible, but Ghost's mother wanted him to have it. So she would quote scripture around him all the time. One she found necessary, especially for a young man was from Proverbs, *above all thy getting's get thee an understanding.* From the first time, Benny Wu heard it, though not impressed with the Bible in whole; he accepted that wisdom.

"I am going to get an understanding?"

"What do I do?"

"Whatever you want."

"I'll sit here and keep the motor running," but she wouldn't sit there long. As soon as he walked to the door, she ran to the window, squatted down and peeped inside.

It was just like she had told him. There were a few chairs and tables, a small dance floor and a couple of pool tables tossed in the back. He thought that it looked a lot like George Ray's in the bottom. They didn't open for a few hours, so the place was empty except for two guys at the bar he assumed were the two Shelia had warned him about. He walked straight up to them "Yes, I'm looking for Mr. Womacky. Could you tell me where I could find him?"

"What business do you have with Womacky?"

They snorted and grinned at each other as if to say check out this punk kid. Neither of them saw the tire iron. For sure the one on the right didn't. If he had, instead of throwing his thumb back at Benny Wu, like the nerve of this guy, he would have been ducking. Because he got it first. A striking blow that cracked splattered and popped his head like a pimple. He fell straight to the floor. His partner was standing in front of him like a mirror as blood splashed him in the face before that horror could set in, Benny Wu hit him in the arm leaving it limp. Then on the opposite side of his body, he brought the bar crashing into his shoulder crushing his collarbone.

The pain in his arms was intense. He wanted to fall to the floor, but Benny was holding him up against the bar. He had hit him in the arm at a 45-degree angle just above the elbow separating the radius and ulna from the humerus, and away from each other. Now they hung limp in his arm like bars of soap in a sock, excruciatingly pulling on the nerve. Benny Wu felt confident that he had removed any stipulations from further communications, but in all fairness, he asked.

"I really don't like people trying to be funny, while I am seriously trying to handle my business. That's the problem I had with your friend; I'm not going to have that problem with you, am I?"

He wanted to say no, but the pain had him in a place where his jaw was just as limp as his arms. However, through it, through the pain, he managed to shake his head no.

Benny Wu said, "We're off to a very good start, now …"

Before he could finish a fat man waddled out of the office, in the back, "What the hell is all this noise about"?

He saw his man stretched out on the floor; the other jacked up, on the bar. He turned to run, but Benny Wu was fast. That extra time it took to swing his girth like his weight was too much. Just out of his turn, Benny Wu caught him with the tire iron. He hadn't taken one good step before the bar smashed square into the side of the knee. It cracked, and the big man came crashing to the floor.

The determined coward still stuck in flight mode, limped halfway to his feet. He was somewhere between hobbling and crawling but firmly on getting the hell out of there, when Benny whapped him across the back. With a hollow thwack, the big man crashed to the ground and surrendered to the dusty floor.

For most people, a good trouncing will suffice, but there are those you have to take to the next level. 'When you need a person to respect your wishes long after you are gone, and not go to the police, you have to implant fear.' The book was very specific on how to accomplish this in The Rules of Intimidation.

First, he had to make the big man believe he wasn't working alone, which wasn't a lie, not now. So when he spoke, he spoke in the plural.

This next part wasn't one of the rules. This was more of a Benny Wu touch; he knew people believed anything that is whispered to them. So he leaned down close to his ear and spoke in a very calm, soft voice, "Shelia is part of our family now. We are assuming all of her debts. That's what I was sent to do; cancel our debts. Let me make sure we are speaking the same language do we owe you anything...else?"

"No, I believe...that caught us...that caught us right up... we...we, we all good..."

Lastly, put a weight on their non-compliance that their soul can't bear.

Benny Wu having a little flair and being a bit of a

salesman felt it was important to make a person feel like they got a good deal. Granted, that was going to be a hard sell when everyone is laid-out on the floor bleeding, but Benny Wu, in the spirit of the 44, gave it a shot, "Look, I am a nice guy, don't make them send a fool...The next time they may start at Ms. Ella May's." That was Womacky's mother.

Benny Wu knew that when they showed up at the hospital, they would have to tell the doctors and police something. The fat man had a fabulous chain with a medallion. It was white gold with a beautiful four-leaf clover with a diamond in each leaf.

"You can tell those folks you got robbed," he said as he took the chain off his neck, "I'm going to take this. To help you, you need to stop believing in luck. This is going to remind you; we make our own destinies. Like, if you all's recollection of the perpetrator is too vivid."

CHAPTER 10

"To thy own self-be true."

Pink was sitting on the bed thinking about Benny Wu when the phone rang. She had never been with anyone like Benny Wu. He had her mind twisted. She wasn't new to sex. By no means was it her first rodeo, but she had never been with anyone like him.

On lovemaking, the Book went into surprising detail on how to keep a woman in your corner. Simple ideas like, always suit up, to the more complex concepts like dicknatizing.

Simplified it is the technique of telling a woman what you need while making love. The idea being women are more acceptable in the throes of passion. Imagine it as positive reinforcement on steroids; it was one of the moves outlined in the section on pimping. Although he had other experiences, it was the first time he had ever tried the technique.

He was a bit aggressive with it, but she came agreeably. With pounding emphasis, he laid out what he wanted, and in waves of ecstasy, she accepted that role. She rose reprogrammed and now could not stop thinking about him, what he said, and how he touched her. He was so inside of her head it was like being made love to from the inside out. She wasn't blind; it was not love. However, whatever he made, he made to her. Special and unique to her, whatever it was to him, and the sound of his voice sent her dripping right back.

"Get somebody to drop you off at that Popeye's by the Bricks. I am going to be there in twenty minutes. Be by yourself." She almost dropped the phone, ended the call and began to scramble. She only had twenty minutes and didn't know how she was going to get there. Even more importantly, what she was going to wear. She had to pick something cute but not too cute.

Summer in Texas, you can't go wrong with shorts. She threw on a pair of cut off blue jeans that fit like skin and a red tank top then started dialing. She went through the entire contact list of girls. Not many of the girls she knew had cars. She went through them fast and started on the boys. She figured it would be a little messy asking a boy to take her to another boy, but whatever.

"Come take me to Popeye's," she left all the rest out; even still she got no. She used the same line on two or three. Then she figured out that most of their problems were they were broke. So she edited it and added in the part about having her own money. One boy said he would if she showed him her poker face. She laughed and hung up the phone, thinking I am not that desperate. Before she could be little herself with a *yet* and set the phone down, it rang. It was Warren.

Every woman has a Warren. He was sweet and would do anything she asked, except leave her alone. He hung around her like a puppy. She would push him away but then would need something. Of course, he would run back just hoping one day her needs will involve coitus.

He was the first guy she had called, but it had gone straight to voicemail.

"Come take me to Popeye's," she blurted out.

"I don't have any money."

"I got my own food."

"I meant gas."

"Come on; I got you on gas."

"You must really want some red beans and rice."

"Boy, you coming or what?"

"Yeah, I am just saying, I think I ought to get a kiss or something for being so nice."

She thought to herself that this boy was for sure a future trick, but his price was still better than the one before.

"You better hurry up and get here before I change my mind."

Warren was there so fast she didn't have time to wait. She gave him five dollars, "You get your kiss when we get there."

Then she thought about it. Even though, she knew it didn't matter. She didn't want Benny Wu to see her kissing him, "Wait" she grabbed his head and kissed him square on the lips. "Now drive!"

Warren hit the gas and screeched off. They were there in no time. Warren pulled up at Popeye's, and Pink hopped out before the car had stopped completely.

"Ok, you can gone on and go."

"Huh?"

"If you can huh, you can hear." it was one of those things her mother said to her all the time. She laughed a little then said. "Naw, I'm just playing, but seriously you can go." She began to scan the parking lot for Benny Wu, "I'm going to get a ride back with a friend."

She didn't see him, so she walked around to the other side of the building, without saying another word to Warren. There she saw Benny Wu getting something out of the trunk of a Chevy Camaro. She walked up on him. "Benny Wu, is this you?" She said pointing to the car.

Benny Wu, who is usually very cool, burst a smile a mile wide. She was so happy for him, she jumped up on him, hugging him. He caught her at the waist and held her a moment then set her down saying, "I need you to take Ghost his car. Go straight down Rittenhouse to Knox." He instructed, "Don't stop anywhere, don't use your phone, and most of all don't speed."

Shelia walked out of the restaurant and straight up to Benny Wu; she put his change into his pocket and looked Pink up and down. She tried to look her in her eyes but didn't say anything.

Pink acknowledged her presence, but never took her eyes off Benny Wu. He had told her that he didn't do 'the girlfriend thing.' So Pink knew whoever this woman was, she had nothing to do with who they were, and besides, she was putting money in his pocket.

Pink only had one question, "Can I wait for you there?",

He started to say he didn't know how long he would be, but realized that didn't matter, "Yeah I need you to; I have something for you."

She was so excited she jumped a bit. He tapped her on her thigh just below her hip and sent her on smiling.

Benny Wu didn't like kissing. He thought it to be infecting. In the movies, people always fall in love after the kiss. As if it was in the mingling of the saliva that the virus spreads. But Shelia needed reassuring and one more push. So he leaned in and kissed her softly on the lips.

Warren had been sitting there watching the entire scene. He had no idea who Benny Wu was but figured he could forget about Pink. He put his car into gear drove two feet and sputtered out of gas.

Ghost was standing in the window when the car pulled through the gate, "Aaawww Benny Wu," he shouted and started heading for the door. Felicia was sitting on the bed, looking curious about his excitement.

Then his phone rings it was Bennie.
Ghost said, "What's up bro? I see you driving through the gate."

"Naw that's my right hand." He knew Shelia would assume he meant partner as in righthand man, but Ghost would understand. "Everything in the trunk is for you but open the Puma box by yourself."

Ghost was a little disappointed. He walked outside; Pink was pushing Lil Eggy back. He was trying to get the keys when Ghost and Felicia came from around the house to the car.

"Benny Wu told me to give the keys to Ghost. I'm not given them to nobody but Ghost. Now move before I tell him."

Felicia noticed that when Lil Eggy heard that he backed away.

Pink turned to Ghost, "Benny told me to give you these." She handed him the keys.

"Thanks."

"He said that I could wait for him here."

"That's cool. Did he say when he would be back?"

"No."

Felicia thought that Pink was dumb just to wait for someone, not knowing how long she would be waiting but decided to stay in her lane, and not say anything. Besides, she was a little shocked to know that they had a thing, but it was obvious Pink had had something.

Shelia sat in the corner curve of the seat, with half her body up against the door. Rocking with the engine, she was flaunting a chance Benny Wu desperately wanted to take.

Deliciously sitting there in the skimpiest outfit that she could find, Shelia had a dare in her eyes that bragged that she had a few moves of her own.

But the number one rule in the book, it was written around the edges of each page, in both English and Latin. La şoara-m-t prâć rescatŭm, to thine own self be true, and he knew from their introduction this relationship would have to be a dead-end.

He pulled into the Enterprise Car Rental on Interstate 45. Benny Wu had parked across the street so that his car would not be caught on camera. He gave her the money to pay for the car, but he didn't go in. As she walked up to him with the keys to the rental in her hand, his plan was to say goodbye, but she spoke first, "Was that your lady?"

"People can't belong to people that's slavery."

He said it as if it were a joke and they both smiled, but she knew he meant that on many levels. She understood them all. She had asked about Pink, but the truth was she didn't care. She wanted Benny Wu so bad; it was whatever. She would accept him under any conditions. As far as she was concerned he could bring the young lady. She believed he was man enough to handle it, at the least, she was woman enough to try.

"I could stay the night leave in the morning."

"I wish you could, but I have so much to do before tomorrow." He didn't tell her it was the first day of school. "Go the way I showed you, and it shouldn't take any more than three or four hours. And I want you to call me as soon as you get home."

She wanted to state her case again but said, "Ok."

She watched him jump in his car and drive off. She watched as the car disappeared around the corner. What she didn't see, just out of her sight, was Benny Wu pulled over and took the SIM card out of the phone and put it into his wallet. And then he threw the phone in the ditch. No, while all of that was going on, she was standing there wondering when she would see Charles again.

It's funny how people can look at the same thing and see completely different things. Ghost popped open the trunk. It was filled with shoes. It was hard not to notice that they were nine and a half. It had been written on a few of the boxes as they came from different hands and in varying places, but enough of them to quickly notice a pattern.

Now Pink, who thought Benny Wu was the most,

saw a trunk full of love, and how the real take care of their people.

Felicia didn't trust Benny Wu and concluded they were stolen. All of Ghost's shoes were size ten. He had told her that he and Benny wore the same size. What she saw was Benny trying to hide them there.

Ghost and Benny were like brothers; one would think he saw a victory. This meant that they were done. The body was gone, Benny Wu had got the money, and they had led all suspicion away from them. What he should have seen was a pocket full of cash and the police chasing a ghost, but he didn't. He saw nine and a half, his real size. He had always bought tens and wore extra socks so that he and Benny could share. What he saw is Benny not needing him anymore. He saw them being torn apart. This the first little rip.

Now Lil Eggy, he was elated because with a couple pairs of socks he just might be able to get into these.

Ghost asked him if he would take them into the house, "Just put them in my room."

He grabbed the blue Puma box, the only tens, and then turned to go into the house. Felicia turned to go with him, but Ghost thought about what Benny Wu had said, "Open it alone!"

There was no telling what was in the box, so he threw a hand up to stop her, "Ah, could you give Eggy a hand? I'll catch up with you guys in a minute." Then turned and walked off. He didn't mean to hurt her feelings, but in his preoccupation, he was very flippant.

Face cracked; she turned to see if Pink had witnessed her dismissal. Pink was laughing. Lil Eggy had an arm full of boxes trying not to look at her, but she had the distinct feeling he was also laughing.

Denny Ray and Tanasha came out of the pool house. Denny Ray started to help Lil Eggy with the shoes, and Tanasha twitched her nose and walked over to Pink. The two giggled off to the pool.

Ghost had no idea what was in the box. Benny had been so unpredictable. Lately, he didn't know what to expect. To be on the safe side, he did as he was told and went to his mother's room. As he passed the bar, he grabbed the Belvedere and took a swig. His nerves settled he opened the box. The shoes were gone. Limited edition Green Lanterns, Benny had those on his feet. In their place, two bundles of hundreds all banded up nice and neat, twenty thousand dollars. Ghost didn't know what to think, but he was definitely relieved. For the first time, he felt like this nightmare was over.

CHAPTER 11

"The fat lady ain't even here."

Tj knew it was the law when he saw the car on the road. It was the tires. The police always have new tires, and theirs were kicking up a dust cloud of Louisiana red clay. Tj was ready. Benny Wu had said they would be coming, "Do just what I told you and didn't add nothing," he remembered his nephew, saying. He thought about his brother and mumbled to himself keep it simple stupid as he wiped his hands and jumped from the porch. He started up the path and was at the gate, by the time she drove up. He was at her car door.

The officer rolled down the window, "Tj Wabasha?"

"Woo-ba-sha" he corrected her.

However, with his thick Cajun accent, it was just as hard to understand. She smiled and got out of the car. She smiled again, as they shook hands. She had on the same suit she wore at Ghost's house. Her dedication to it caused her to keep it a size too long, but she had not noticed how tight it had gotten. Not until he started looking at her, like she was the last pork chop.

"Sorry, bout your pretty suit," he said as he unconsciously licked his lips and wiped his mouth. "It ain't rained in months. I am afraid it's going to get all dusty."

"This old thing, please, I am about to eat my way out of it."

"I shoal would like to be there for that last bite, you know, when you go to popping out."

Normally she would put him in his place. Let him know in the harshest way possible she didn't find his flirtation amusing, but like all cops, she had done a background check, before she came out there. She had gotten his prison records and had read his psychiatric evaluation. That is why she came alone. From his profile, she knew if she tried to intimidate him by a show of any force, he would reciprocate by shutting down. She needed him to be just a little off balance. The suit was an accident she mildly regretted. After all it was working for her, so instead of letting him have it, she smiled again and told him why she was there.

Tj gave her the account of what happened. It went off perfectly, but she knew it would. The perpetrator was one step ahead of her at every turn. When she went to place a warrant on his truck, it popped up; he had just sold it. She checked the title and the transfer, but they were perfect. The lab confirmed the signatures. Tj confirmed the story. She put a freeze on his bank account, but again, he beat her to the punch. The morning she got the court order, he had just left the bank. Everywhere she turned was a dead end. Tj had said exactly what she thought he would. She had one chance left, the reason she had driven for four hours. The one question she had to ask him in his face.

"What made him come here?" The idea was to catch

him off guard. Then toss out some improbable scenario, and hope he reached for something that could not be verified. All she had to do was catch him in one lie, "Did you run an ad in the paper?"

He didn't reach, because he wasn't desperate. Benny Wu had prepared will, "I don't know," he said as if he had not expected the question. "I had been telling folks round here, that I was looking for a good truck since I got my settlement. I figured one of them sent him. I ain't gone lie; it was a nice truck. I didn't even ask."

It was just like Benny Wu said. All he had to do now was send her on her away.

"Sorry I couldn't be of more help," he said like that was it.

But she felt like he was hiding something, and she was about to find out. It went against everything she believed, as a feminist, as a cop, and as a woman but she put aside her police training, disregarded the psychical evaluation and she looked him in his eyes and said, "Not as sorry as I am." Then she dropped her head as if she could not handle the sorrow, turning it slightly as if she could not bear the shame, then she saw it. Out of the corner of her eye; she saw him raise his hand just a little, to reach for her. He pulled it back, but she had already seen it. He had felt her desperation, and she knew as long as she kept him right there, he would mistake it for his own.

"Please Sir, you have to give me something." She said as she grabbed his arm pulling at it desperately.

Now Benny had told him, specifically, "Don't add anything!" but he didn't see any harm in given this beautifully desperate woman some hope. Benny hadn't told him anything about Theodore Mason but his name, but in his distaste for him, Benny referred to him as a pervert. So his uncle added, "The young lady he was with had on one of those Madisonville High T-shirts. Maybe she was from around there."

Benny had told him to tell the police he had dropped Barry off at the Dairy Queen by the Grey Hound station, but his uncle figured he would give her a little hope. She would hustle off up to Madisonville. Drive around a while and give the disappointment time to sink in.

"Young lady?" Detective DeValo said excitedly.

He was lying. He hadn't mentioned a young lady before, but that wasn't it. From everything that she had gathered on the perpetrator, his propensity was young boys, and if he were with a woman, it would be an older woman, he could use.

"Yeah, I didn't get a good look at her. She parked over there, but when she got in the passenger seat as they were leaving, I could see for sho it was a young woman." He was proud of his lie, but she could smell it.

"Is there anything else that you think might help me find this man?" She knew he would say no. His no was irrelevant, a formality, part of the setup. It was all about the next question. "Is there another number I can reach you at?"

He thought about what Benny Wu had said don't give then anything that links to me. In the court where they had transferred the title, Benny made sure his uncle didn't use his cell number saying, "I called you from home on this phone three days ago." That's how Benny Wu knew he had the money, "don't use this number on nothing official."

So he said no quickly.

This time she knew he was lying. Even crackheads have cell phones. She pushed him, "What, a ladies' man like yourself?" However, she could have pushed all she wanted; he was done. He knew he had made a mistake. He messed up somehow; someway he said too much. However, he had a plan to fix it, "If that's all Miss." He turned and walked off without knowing if it was or not.

Ghost walked off leaving Felecia standing in the driveway. She was livid at the way she had been treated. She already felt like Pink could be harboring a little animosity behind her friend Keyanda and then Ghost shined on her like she was a groupie. Feeling completely embarrassed, she continued her thought with 'If he thinks that I am going to sit around here like Pink and the rest of them dizzy, dumb females waiting for him, he has another thought coming.' She jumped into her car and buckled up and drove off.

Ghost was at the window. He saw her pulling off and grabbed his phone. She was pulling through the gate, by the time he dialed the number and was turning the corner before she answered the phone. Her thought was to let him have it, but something inside of her wanted to say, "Oh, I was just going to the store," then she could come back like nothing had happened.

Ghost was still listening for her voice on the phone when Benny Wu drove through the gate. He couldn't see the person driving, but he knew it was Benny Wu.

The Camaro pulled through with such force that it had to be Benny Wu. It was a fiercely dark gray that laid flat under the shine. With absolutely no chrome against the darkening evening sky, it seemed to be sucking in the light.

Benny Wu came across it while he was trying to find a bank. It was primed out, on the side of the road with a few other cars in front of this salvage yard. Unlike the others, there was no price on the windshield. Instead, it read buyer pick your color. Benny Wu had looked at it for a long moment before he walked in.

"How much for the Camaro?"

There were two guys inside. The one leaning on the counter looked out the window, saw the BMW, and straightened up. Then he said, "Have you taken a good look at her?" He grabbed the key and small yellow book off the shelf.

"Let me stop you right there."

The middle-aged man looked a bit confused.

"I see you have the book," Benny Wu was referring to the Kelly Blue Book that lists the fair market value of vehicles, "so I know where you're going on that. However, the car is primed out, so you probably have a salvage title on it." The guy twisted his face a little.

Benny Wu said, "Cool, so you know where I am going with this."

He was acknowledging that he was aware that the car had been totaled. Although it was nicely refurbished, no bank will finance a salvage title. Whoever bought that car had to have cash!

"What do you want for the car?"

He looked Benny Wu up and down. His plan was to have the person sit in the car. The interior had been re-tucked in this lime green that had been salvaged when they renovated the elementary school. His dad told him to use it because it was free. Despite his father's lack of care, he did a wonderful job. It was hard to get the entire feel because of the tint. In fact, you couldn't even see the color unless you were looking through the windshield, and Benny had. He looked through that windshield and at every seam.

Benny knew cars, as a child that was one of his first hustles, washing cars. He would hang out at the car wash on West Montgomery and Little York. He started drying cars for tips. He worked his way up to his own bucket, shammy, Armor All, and five fragrances of Bam before the dope heads, and winos ran him off. Hustling is like the stage; a kid will outshine you every time, but he learned a lot, scrubbing on cars and listening to lies. Like how to spot scanty bodywork. He learned that the history of a car is in the seams. There you will find where it has been hit. What type of work has been done to it and what type of mechanic did the job. He had looked at every seam. It would take a fractional caliper to know it had ever been wrecked. It was perfect.

That's why he wanted Benny Wu to sit in the car. Get the feel of the vehicle. Start the engine; let it purr, while he showed him the books estimated value in mint condition. However, Benny Wu wouldn't play ball, at least not his game.

Most consumers make the mistake of assuming that the deal is about the product they are purchasing. However, every product from the moment it is conceived is designed to get the money out of your pocket. Benny Wu never took his mind off his money.

"Once we paint it, it will be worth 21 or 22, but I'll let you have it for 18."

"I was going to offer you 12 as is, but if you are going to paint it, I will give you 14."

"I wasn't negotiating I want 18." He was so stern; Benny threw up his hands in surrender.

"Ok then. I didn't mean to waste your time. You'll

have a good day," Benny Wu said and turned to walk out.

The man's father stepped from behind the wall and said to Benny Wu, "Hold up son."

He was an old man, but his presence was strong. He looked Benny Wu up and down, and then he turned back and looked at his son, then back to Benny Wu, "You serious bout da car out dar' we nar' through negotiating."

His accent was so thick; Benny wasn't sure about what the man had said. However, he heard car and serious, so he pulled out a wad of cash, "I wasn't looking for a car today but this is four thousand, and I can go get the rest."

He looked at his son with a slight disappointment. The boy just didn't get it. His father had made the case so many times.

Just like people once lived off the river, they live off the highway. They had a tremendous advantage. Their fishing hole was a wrecker and towing service with a salvage yard and body shop that sit smack dab in the middle of a badly engineered curve and a poorly lit railroad crossing. But that doesn't mean anything if his son didn't know what to do, once he had a fat fish on the hook.

The man noticed Benny Wu's face tighten slightly, and he smiled. He recognized Benny's type. This boy is a muddy water catfish he thought.

Now, when you are fishing for catfish that are used to swimming in muddy water, you can't keep casting your line and getting all fancy with it. They will not bite at anything moving fast through that dirty water. You can't do a muddy water catfish the way you do a trout flicking the bait in its face, and then snatching it away. That just gone aggravate him, he will hit your line so hard, he'll steal the bait if it rips his lip. Naw, for a muddy water catfish what you do is just put it in front of him. If he wants it, all you have to do is leave a little slack in the line. Once he peers through that muddy water and sees what he wants, he's going to hit it. He is going to hit it fast and run with it. You don't even have to pull your pole as soon as he runs out of slack, that hook will catch. Some catfish have swallowed the bait so deep; they had to cut the hook out of its stomach.

"It was just that Sir, I like the color." It was all primed dark gray. "I know that's prime, but I like that flatness. What if I brought you nine and you don't paint it." Benny Wu asked.

The old man smiled, "If that's what you like son, I know just what you want, but you gone bring me back twelve."

It was lacquer. He had six, and a half gallons of black lacquer paint that were left over from the refurbishing of some vintage police cars they had done six or seven years ago. He added the rest of the white that he had. The result was a dark smoke gray that laid flat like the color on one of those old Match Box cars. It was better than any of them could have hoped.

Now it was pulling through the gate. Ghost had forgotten that he was on the phone he reached and opened the window and shouted out, "Hey Benny!"

Felicia could hear him over the phone and knew that she had lost that round. There was no use in making a big scene, "No I am fine I just have school in the morning, I need to get ready… Yes, I am sure …Ok …Ok…Ok bye."

Everyone was standing around the car by the time Ghost got downstairs. Parked ace duce it purred in the driveway its color so deep it seemed like you could stick your hand into it.

"What is that color?" Lil Eggy said like he wanted to touch it.

"It's Fuzzy Black." Benny Wu opened the door, and the lime green exploded into the night.

Denny Ray shouted, "Man dem ho's fina go crazy."

They painted the rims the same color as the car. It made the car look like Benny Wu. It looked hungry and angry. It looked as if, had it fists; they would be balled. However, tonight Benny didn't harbor the animosity, it was Ghost. He was smiling and congratulating his friend, but inside he felt something he had never felt before, he was jealous.

CHAPTER 12

"It warmed the ground, so I grew toward that."

Getting back to school was good for everybody. It allowed them to fall back into their old routines. Benny didn't drive his car. He didn't want it to coincide with Barry leaving. Patiently he was waiting for a proper time to unveil it. That too worked out for the best. Riding around with his buddy like they used to, helped Ghost to quell his jealousy, and the extra attention from Benny Wu helped to fill the void.

Unfortunately, he hadn't seen Felicia much since school started, and it was driving him crazy. They talked on the phone nightly and would text during the day, but it wasn't enough. He missed her. She blamed it on the campaign, the fact it was senior year, and on top of all that her job. Ghost accepted her excuses but Benny Wu, he didn't say anything to his friend, but he knew that wasn't altogether the truth. Benny knew Felecia threw herself in the campaign to take up her time.

For those who don't know, Acres Homes is a political powerhouse. Economically diverse, there are both Democrats and Republicans, so Obama created a unique situation. Being the first African American seriously vying for the White House Acres Homes was pulsating. Naturally, you had your Democrats beating the campaign drum, but there were Republicans who secretly supported him as well. Not to mention those Republicans who didn't but had the good common sense to acknowledge that no black person was going to vote against Obama. They pushed the idea that you don't have to vote straight ticket to be on the right side of history.

If you ever find yourself driving down Ella Boulevard when you cross over Tidwell, the street turns into Wheatley, named after Phyllis Wheatley, you have entered Acres Homes. Now if you go just a piece farther and look on the right, you would see the Beulah Ann Shepard Building. You will know it when you see it because Mrs. Shepard's signature is on the side of the building. It is a beautiful six-foot sign in bright red. That's pretty much how Mrs. Shepard was in life. If she put her name on it, it was official. The building is home to the Acres Homes Chamber Of Commerce, and there is no one greater they could have chosen to honor. Beulah Ann Shepard was more than a matriarch; she was the reason for the word. It might be hard to believe that an uneducated black woman would hand pick senators and congressman, but she did. Her legacy is a politically mobilized community with an extremely loud voice. Ask anyone, President Bush, Governor Perry, if you wish to do anything in Texas politics you must come through Acres Homes.

Mrs. Shepard was old then, very old, but the machine that she helped to put into place was oiled and ready for this moment. For most African Americans, it was an exciting time, but in Acres Homes, it was a call to arms. Benny Wu knew what Felicia knew, they didn't need her, but once she threw herself into that machine; they'd keep her hopping like a frog on hot dirt.

He was right. She was put off by the way Ghost acted. Then there was the whole thing with the shoe box. The way he got it and all secretly ran off. There are a lot of drug dealings in Acres Homes, and she would have no part of that, but she liked Ghost, so rather than say anything, she just kept him at a distance. You can see better from a distance and sometimes what the heart needs is room to grow.

But being back at school had the most profound effect on Lil Eggy. It wasn't just the clothes, although, it was nice to have clothes that fit. Felicia bought his uniform pants from a Japanese wholesaler that she found online. Japanese people are small. Still, she had to do some alterations, but she knew clothes and was a good seamstress, so he looked nice. She had updated his look a bit placed him somewhere between prep and skater. He felt a little odd at first, but the girls made it easy. All the time they talked to him, they rubbed on his clothes and smiled; he smiled back. That didn't happen back when he smelled like Dial anti-bacterial soap. Now that he was splashing on Channel Blue it was a whole new party, but he was not invited. He was the host!

Everywhere he sat a circle of girls sat around him. Even his teachers noticed and took deeper breaths when they were near him and gave him extra smiles and nods. He didn't have to worry about extra socks; there was plenty of cash floating around, and when Benny Wu gave him and Denny Ray their part of the money the first thing Lil Eggy did was buy him some shoes, his own size.

He looked like something he never looked like

before, someone with money. However, it was more than that. It was his confidence. It was through the roof, but it wasn't the money, clothes or the girls. It was the family.

Ms. Marry was a good woman. She provided a safe enough place for him to lay his head, but she was old and not a mother. Her house, nice as it was, wasn't home. It was a foster home. And so many kids, with so many problems, had been paraded through there, it felt more like a hotel for the future's perverse. Every relationship he had there was loose, and its only redeeming quality was that it would be temporary.

But none of that mattered anymore. He wasn't alone anymore. He had a family now. He had been by himself, but now he belonged to something, something great.

Benny Wu didn't think a name was important at first but soon began to understand that once you name something, it begins to become alive. Every time you called its name, it grows until it's a wanting, needing, living thing, and he did. He called the name often, and though they represented it in secret, he made sure they called it often too. They breathed life into the Disciples of Judas pledging to do whatever evil was necessary, and that beast breathed a confidence in Lil Eggy that was shining like the sun.

There is only one problem with brilliance, everybody wants to shine, and with Lil Eggy so bright, it wouldn't be long before someone tried to put his little lamp out.

Honestly, as far as middle school squabbles go these days, it was nothing. Some bigger kid tired of Lil Eggy getting all the attention, big faced him in the restroom. His hand nearly covered Lil Eggy's whole head as he pushed him to the filthy restroom floor. Lil Eggy jumped up to fight him, but just then a teacher walked in.

They could have let it go, let the school handle it. However, Benny Wu saw it as a chance to give Lil Eggy the last thing he needed. To turn Lil Eggy into the beast, Benny Wu needed him to be, power.

They were leaving Booker T. Washington driving down Yale when Benny Wu got the call from Lil Eggy in the principal's office.

"This is what I want you to do….Ghost, turn right up here."

"Are you sure?" Lil Eggy said trying not to sound unsure.

"Yeah, Eggy, do it just like I told you."

Detective DeValo was at a complete loss. Everywhere she turned, it was a dead end. She had gone through Tj's phone records at his house. There was one call she was sure was from the perpetrator. It was at the right time. Whoever that was that called Tj, was calling someone in Houston, but they stopped using those phones. But there was nothing that linked Tj to anyone in Houston.

Ironically, she walked into the bank feeling like she was chasing a ghost. She met the teller who introduced her to the manager, Shelia.

Detective DeValo thought that she was an attractive woman but dressed a little too young.

Her judgmental stares made Shelia feel a little uncomfortable, and subconsciously, she tugged at her skirt.

To the point, the detective told Shelia why she was there, "I am sure you remember."

Shelia said she didn't, but she did. She was not able to get Benny Wu off of her mind. Even now, when her focus should be on potential peril, she was fantasizing. Thoughts of him pulsated through her. She could almost taste his sweaty, salty, chocolate skin.

In the throes of her fantasy, true to the character she knew she would have to play, she pretended to be offended by the detective's assumption and asked, "Why are you sure I would remember because we are in the country."

She said in a manner that made the detective feel embarrassed by her postulation. It was evident in her reaction.

"It's ok," Shelia said in her highest pitched voice as she moved to her computer.

"It's a common mistake because we are out here in the middle of nowhere."

Then she began to get ditzier with every word, "I know a lot of people would be surprised to realize how much cash we deal with, but each home out here is a business. You would be amazed how many of their transactions are done in cash. I think to keep the government out of the business, but that's not my business, you know. "

She looked over the paper again at the account number as if she didn't remember. Then went right back to what she was saying, "Just about every land deal, you know. It ain't my place to say. Oh here we go, yes I remember."

Shelia went through the entire story of the morning; Detective DeValo found the woman so draining she wanted to scream. She was in a sorority and had one or two sisters who could be trying but, "My God" she thought "This woman runs a bank."

She could not tell if she was this ditzy for real or if

this was just a cover.

The main problem with teaching someone how to spot crime, you also teach them how to commit it. And Shelia did everything perfectly. She wore three pairs of latex gloves. To disguise the swing, she used a weighted felt tip pen, and it was perfect. As she knew it must be.

"Ms. Monroe if this is so common place, how do you remember this withdrawal so well?"

Shelia was already tired, and with the accusatory remark, it was time to stop the games. The ditzy game she was playing and the strong-arm game Detective DeValo was trying to startup.

"Because that was the day the cameras went out," Shelia informed the detective.

"I am going to need another number on you in case we need to talk again," the detective said to Shelia, but she was already stretching across the desk for the card. She handed it to the detective, "If there is nothing else," she stood up and pointed at the door.

"But there is one more thing," DeValo said.

Studewood and Acres Homes are sisterhoods. They are divided by Shepherd Boulevard. Before they annexed Acres Homes, the city of Houston had a substation that set smack dab on the Boulevard. The Houston Police use to patrol it like a border. After the Annex, to combat the growing drug problems in Acres Homes, the City abandoned the Shepherd station and built a massive substation in the heart of Acres Homes on West Montgomery. But still almost 40 years later, among most of the hustlers, the line surprisingly still exists. Now a junkie will go anywhere to buy drugs. They buy drugs in jail, but for the most part, among the hustlers, neither side crosses the line. But Benny Wu claimed the earth as his turf. He had grown up everywhere and had gone to school with everyone. He knew all of them, from the BGs (baby gangsters) to the old-school players, no matter how down or how lame; he knew them. Kids his age didn't even know players like Eric and Chris Vosie from the Nickel, but his mother had been dragging him around dope houses all his life.

Most people in Houston don't even know where the Sixth Ward is, but his mother would drop him off in the park, while she smoked at the Hobbit House. He was eight-years-old running for the players Calvin Dillard and Chunky Blue. He knew everybody, and since he was already on that side of Shepherd, on Yale when he told Ghost to turn right, they pulled on to Hohldale St.

There were two kids born on Hohldale named Peter. No child wants to be called Peter. So it wasn't long before people went to calling them, Pete. That gets confusing, and in the south, people like it simple, so you had Big Pete and Skinny Pete.

Big Pete was a youth minister at Mount Olive Baptist Church. He drove a truck for Mrs. Baird's. They drove straight past his house. Pulled in down by the dead end and hopped out at Skinny Pete's. He ran a crew of BGs. They called themselves The Hohldale Boyz.

Lil Eggy put his phone into his pocket and walked into Principal McDuff's office. The other young man in the altercation JaMicheal was sitting in a chair in front of the desk. He looked at Principal McDuff, then at JaMicheal, then back to the principal. But he could see Benny Wu in face time, hear his voice echoing inside his head, "Do it just like, I said."

"Principal McDuff, before we get started, I need to apologize to JaMicheal." He turned his attention to the young man twice his size, who looked quite befuddled. "This isn't your fault. I am not used to having things. I know I have been getting on people's nerves." Looking JaMicheal directly in the eyes he said earnestly, "I'm really sorry." Then he stuck his hand out just like Benny Wu said.

JaMicheal didn't know how to take it. He was confused but stood up and shook Lil Eggy's hand, "It's cool."

"Sir," Lil Eggy said to Principal McDuff, "there is no reason to hold JaMicheal. This is my doing, and if I can speak to you for a moment alone, I am sure I can clear the rest of this up for you."

Normally, he would just give both of them detention and be done with it but he was interested to see what the young man would say next.

"Is that true son, are we done with this?" he said to JaMicheal, who quickly said yes sir and skirted out the door.

His two classmates waiting for him outside the office laughed and clowned as they walked out of the building and up Knox Street heading toward the grocery store Orlando's.

Now it was time to wrap it up with Principal McDuff. From The Book '*Wear gloves whenever you can, and when you can't, don't touch anything, you're not taking with you. Wear a mask because you can wrap up your witnesses, but that camera is never scared to testify. When it comes to evidence, all the trails lead to jail.'*

He could walk out of the door not get any punishment, but if there was a record of the incident, Benny Wu would consider that a failure. After all that Benny Wu had done for Lil Eggy, he would die before disappointing him.

Lil Eggy looked at the report in the principal's hand and said, "Sir, I am in foster care, and if I start getting bad reports I may have to move. I really like it here. I have a job, and Ms. Marry is a nice lady. She warned me about showing off."

People love to have something to hold over your head. Lil Eggy could see that once again Benny Wu was right. He had given the principal something to dangle. Knowing the young man's carrot made him comfortable, so when Lil Eggy told him, he would never have a problem out of him again, he accepted that was the truth.

"Oh, I believe you but what about JaMicheal."

"Sir I really don't believe he is going to be a problem."

JaMicheal and his friends crossed the street in the front of Noc's grandmother's house. Even the most ruthless in Acres Homes respected the Gangster Noc, and it was a well-known fact that he didn't tolerate any nonsense around his grandmother's house. When it came to her, he considered everything dealing with humans that moved the air nonsense, and that went from selling dope to giggling.

As they approached the Multi-Purpose Center, this little kid walked up to them and asked which one of them was J-Mac. The skinny boy walking behind JaMicheal spoke, "Why in the hell you wanna know?"

112

From out of nowhere a hand slapped the side of his face so hard, the fleshy inside of his jaw smashed into his teeth, sending blood and spittle flying from his mouth. He squinted to cry and pointed up and out at JaMicheal as the tears leaped from his eyes. However, his snitching really didn't play a role. There were already two guys profusely beating JaMicheal, and little dudes were still climbing out of the Dodge like it was a clown car. It was so feverish Benny began to have mixed feelings. He wanted a message delivered to the little dudes but felt this might be overkill.

Benny Wu was standing on Noc's grandmother's porch. He motioned to Pete to go ahead deliver the message. He was already standing there trying to remember it the way Benny Wu had said it, all smooth and elegant, but couldn't quite put it all together. All the time the little dudes were getting river danced on. Pete figured he better make up something before they got stomped into butter. The one thing Benny Wu said that he did remember was say, it in his ear.

Pete kind of misunderstood leaned down to the boy who had a foot on his neck and shouted, "From now on Lil Eggy is yo' God. You better start looking out for him. Cause fuck if you touch him, if anybody touches him, we coming to see you. But next time we brang dem pistols to the party and are inviting your people." He pulled back his shirt and showed the Glock 45 in his waist. Inspired by all of the uniforms Skinny Pete concluded, "Anybody don't understand what I said or thank I'm bullshitting raise your hand."

Of course, no one did, just like the Geechees back in La Fontaine they were gripped with fear.

Fear is a gangster's greatest ally. It is both sword

and shield. The latter stamped with a caveat that is not to be ignored, but to Benny's defense, he had never seen fear fail. For him, it was the reason for everything. The reason men build shelters, their fear of the cold. They build fences for fear of their neighbors and guns for fear of their foes. Fear had built men and destroyed nations. His entire life he had been washed in fear, either he was afraid or frightening.

It was his tenth birthday. He had gotten a bike. It was significant because he never got anything for his birthday. Like those families who instead of Christmas do Income Tax, he never got anything on the day. It was made more special because it was the first time he got something they didn't take back. He learned the secret to keeping in poverty, the only way to have in hell. This time fear pushed him into the deep end without his water wings; this time he learned to swim.

Although he was barely clothed and often hungry, crackhead or not his mother kept him relatively safe, away from predators and the like. She had a steady, trick, Mr. Jessie. Of all her men friends he was Benny's favorite. He was nice. She cleaned the house when he was coming over, and he always had a few dollars in his pockets for the boy. He had bought him a bike for his birthday, in hindsight it was good he did.

Benny always wondered why a guy, as nice and so cool didn't have a wife and family. He didn't understand being broken, but Mr. Jessie was broken.

Like a pipe, you can't tell where the cracks are until you turn on the water. Mr. Jessie was a bit of a drinker, and when he got drunk, he was somewhat of a bully.

Well, that's common for men who feel small in their real life. Anyway, this day overfed by a bonus, the liquor grew this bully into a tyrant. He started screaming and hollering. Bennie's mother shooed Benny into a closet, to shield him from the anger while she tried to calm the beast.

Under a pile of dirty clothes, muffled by his own sobbing the child, cried himself to sleep.

Wrapped in the dark, balled into a knot, all things breaking sound the same, he woke because of a rare smell, food cooking. He sprang from the closet and ran to the kitchen. His mother motioned for him to keep quiet, but he was making a 'B' line to the stove. The house was clean, so it was hard to tell which things were broken or merely propped up. Plus, he was hungry.

It is ironic that impoverished neighborhoods are often labeled food deserts, being most poor often have a camel type mentality when it comes to food. Whenever they get a chance to eat, they fill their humps. He looked up from the stove expecting to her to beam with pride, but what he saw was her eye, bruised and swollen, nearly closed, the skin so tight it looked as if it would pop. He stopped where he was. He looked at his mom confused and simultaneously shook. He began to look around the room; the furniture mended, propped and pushed together.

Horrifically, his mind went in rewind and added Mr. Jessie, a man he had come, to admire demonstratively destroying his house and mother's face. He was so frightened, but this time fear pushed him to the other side. He grabbed the knife from the table.

"Baby no..." his mother thought but didn't say anything. Instead, she watched him. Then she grabbed the other knife and stuck it into her pocket. Prepared to do for her child what she wouldn't do for herself.

Benny walked into the room where Mr. Jessie lay

sleeping. He stood beside the bed as he did when he asked for money. Although underfed, for his age he was very strong. He woke Mr. Jessie. When he had come to and saw the boy standing beside the bed, he smiled as if nothing had happened. When Benny was convinced Mr. Jessie was wide awake, Benny put the knife to his neck. He pressed the knife so tight it forced his head against the headboard. Jessie was pent. He had to breathe shallow not to get cut, "If you ever put your hands on my mama again instead of waking you up, I will cut your throat from ear to ear…I cross my heart and hope to die."

Mr. Jessie unable to speak or nod but was bucked eyed blinking in an agreeable fashion. He was scared, and Benny could see it in his eyes, and smell it in his nose. Jessie had been drinking all night and with fear squeezing on his bladder; he had to let that liquid courage go.

His money lay on the night stand. That was one of those old-school wanna be a pimp moves, 'bitch bet not touch my money.'

It wasn't but forty-seven dollars, but with his other hand, Benny Wu took it. The first thing he learned in school was if they are scared smash on the gas, "I am going to get me something to eat. I don't want your food, and I don't want you here when I get back," he walked toward the door then gave the knife to his mother, "And Mr. Jessie, I don't want to see you here as long as my Mama looks like that."

People wonder how a man becomes a pimp. Sometimes it is because their Mamas were their first whores. He hopped on his bike and road, to Popeye's and bought a three-piece with red beans and rice, to this day his celebratory meal, vowing forever to be the bigger badder beast.

CHAPTER 13

"Be careful about what you ask for."

It has been debated since the first time they took a bone and stitched together two pieces of hide. Does the woman make the dress or does the dress make the woman? Felicia stepped out of her Honda Accord fiercely, in a white lace Nicole Miller that set the debate vigorously raging on. She knew in the mirror it was a bit much for a high school party, but her man was hosting that made her queen bee, and half the joy of being queen was sending the lesser bees buzzing. Plus, she and Ghost had argued the last time they were together, so if in any way he started up her plan was to walk next door to The Blue Room. It was grown folks, but the way she looked; they weren't going to check her ID.

Tonight she was going to party and felt no guilt about it. She wanted to go somewhere looking so good that every man's mouth was wide open, and wearing something so bad every woman was talking about it. She had it made up in her mind; tonight every tongue was going to testify.

She walked to the front of the house where the girls were gathered.

"Ah, Bitch that dress is hot to death," Pink chimed as she sauntered around the car.

"I know hum!" she spun around so that she could see the rest of the dress.

"Bitch looks like she's going to the prom," Keyanda spitefully hurled into the conversation.

Felicia expected hate from Keyanda. She knew she was jealous, just like she knew that Keyanda was the one who called T-Mobile and turned off her phone, and then the Internet gangster hacked her Facebook account. She changed the password, locking Felicia out and for two days, posted raunchy lies fueled with multiple sexual partners ranting about drug use and a grateful miscarriage.

Keyanda was getting pretty and polite confused, with scared and won't fight. Despite being dead wrong, Felicia let it go. Already resolved one funky monkey wasn't going to stop her show.

She did just what she was supposed to do. She wouldn't even get involved in Keyanda's nonsense. She treated her like a little girl and did not even acknowledge the unruly child. But Tanasha and her friend Chalice had ridden with Felicia. Chalice, knowing just how foul Keyanda had been, turned to Felicia and said, "Some hoes can't pull off classy!"

The girls erupted in laughter. Felicia chuckled a bit at seeing Keyanda put into her place but became put off by the volume of the laughter.

Felicia thought it would be best if she just left. So she walked on, heading into the house. She didn't look Keyanda in the eyes, because she didn't want to start any trouble, but she didn't hold her head down because she wasn't scared.

That move cut Keyanda deeper than the flippant line. Keyanda took it as a continuance of her dismissal. She assumed that Ghost had told Felicia what had happened between them, but he didn't. He wouldn't even tell the police. But when the other girl called her, a whore that's how Ghost made her feel.

He had retreated. It was so different from how it had been. Keyanda felt he must have told Felicia. Keyanda felt violated and betrayed, but even worse than his dismissal was Felicia's.

Looking at Felicia, she felt worthless, used and soon she would be thoughtlessly discarded, like one of those cheap napkins you'd find in a gas-station restroom. Wadding her up tighter and tighter, the obsessive laughing forced her to a resolution. At that moment, Keyanda resolved, she would not be ignored. She balled-up her fist tight, bit down and swung with all of her might.

Felicia knew Keyanda was sneaky and was watching her out of the corner of her eye. She had a plan. She had mapped it out before she took a step. All of the girls at St. Pious take karate as part of that good private school education. She had been practicing waiting for a chance to use it. Now it was coming.

She had it all figured out. First what she was going to do was, in one motion with her purse still in her hands, grabbed the bottom of her dress pull it up a little. It cost too much to bust up for Keyanda. Then she would take her 4-1/2 inch heel and with a side thrust, kick the trifling tramp in her upper thigh. Then when she hollered and bent to grab her leg, she would take the front of the foot, not the heel, she didn't want to scar her for life, just smack her in the face, and knock her to the ground and up out of her business.

It didn't go anything like that!

Keyanda swung, aiming for Felicia's head. Felicia turned to drop into her stance to kick Keyanda, but her back heel broke. She collapsed onto the ground, and Keyanda went flying pass her into Benny Wu's arms.

Felicia had never seen Benny Wu but knew who he was immediately. This is a fine specimen of a man, she thought. To say he was either sexy or cute would demean his appeal. To her, he was beautiful, magnificently beautiful. There was this strength about him. It was in all of him, in his face, his arms even the way he smiled was strong. Felicia was staring up at him from the ground making him appear taller, but she could tell he was tall. Keyanda was struggling to get free, but he held her effortlessly. So much so that Felicia was slow about getting up. He was trying to defuse the situation, meaning calming Keyanda down. He was eloquent, but soon tired of diplomacy, "Pink, make sure nothing happens to that girl!" he said referring to Felicia.

Pink said it like it was a joke. Her voice was light and airy as she glanced across the crowd, "Don't worry Benny Wu awn-one of them touch her; they got to see me." Then she looked directly at Keyanda and said, "Awn-one!"

Keyanda was still struggling, but Benny Wu knew she was scared of Pink. So he let her go, pushing her toward Felicia a little. Keyanda took two small steps trying not to fall then stopped in that spot. She was hot but she wasn't melted, because they couldn't have poured Keyanda on Felicia.

"You are supposed to be investigating a sexual predator, not a murderer," her captain insisted. "Well, if it's a murder pass it to homicide."

She didn't say anything because she didn't have anything. Anything he would go on. Her captain was a quiet man, who could handle the work load, but the stress of the politics weighed on him. There was a time he would have backed a young officer trying to do what's right, but his hair was thinning. He was tired, and with his pension on the horizon, he played a game with no fouls. "What do you have?" he asked the detective.

"A gut feeling."

"Let me make sure I have this straight. You want me to take your guts to the DA?" When he said that way, it sounded silly, but she paid him no attention and kept going.

"I think Marcus killed his step-father, then after sending us chasing a ghost, he high-tailed it up to Louisiana and cleaned out the bank account."

"I know what you think. I asked. What do you have?"

She had nothing. She knew that the Cajun was lying, but a lie is the truth unless you can catch it. All the Cajun's papers were straight. That was the same problem she had at the bank everything was in order. However, there was one gem. The bank's ATM camera caught a glimpse of Marcus's car.

"I have a picture of Marcus's car at a gas station across the street from the bank."

She showed him the clip.

"This car is the exact same color and style."

"But you can't even see the license plate, what do

you want me to do with this?"

"I need to check the house bring forensics back in. If we could just check for blood; there had to be a struggle!"

"Let me stop you right there. That's not going to happen."

"Marcus killed his stepfather. I know it."

"Look that will be a media mess. I will have lost my job before the ink is dry on the warrant. You bring me something concrete a body or witness, anything that connects that boy to bank. Hell if you can just prove he was in Louisiana at the time the perp withdrew the money, we'll arrest him.

Then you can take your time, we can go over the house with a fine-tooth comb, but otherwise, the cases on your desk are stacking up." She was at a dead end. She had been running the traffic cameras all over Louisiana, but that was going to prove futile. Benny Wu had bought temporary license plates from the Jamaicans on Mount and put them on the BMW before he had left Houston.

When Benny Wu went back into the house, Felicia followed him. She asked where Marcus had gone, knowing that he and the other guys had gone to have their rings sized, but she wanted to talk and needed a place to start a conversation. Benny knew that Ghost had already told her where he was going, but didn't say anything.

He told her about the rings, "This guy was selling this piece and chain. It was kind of tacky, but the stones were nice, so we all had rings made."

Just like he knew she had lied. She knew that was a

lie. No one gets a ring made the wrong size. His was the only one that fit. He had them all made, but just like he let it go; she let it go, instead of commenting on what she thought was modesty she gave her attention to the ring. It was a three-carat pink diamond set in sterling silver.

"It's magnificent!"

"Thank you" he replied simply.

His thank you surprised her as did everything else about him. He was nothing that she had thought. He was smarter, much smarter, but it wasn't that. It was the way he studied her. He seemed to be taking her apart, examining her bit by bit. It was nerve-racking in a very sensual way. He seemed to radiate this hunger that made it hard for her to concentrate. For the first time, she knew how people felt when they met her, "Benny Wu is that your real name."

Normally, Benny didn't run around telling his government name, but he wanted them to be cool. Ghost was his best friend, and he was really into her. To him, it was important that they be friends or at least friendly. Not that Ghost was a mark, but he was the kind that would choose a female over his boys. So, for now, everybody had to be cool with each other.

He was less impressed with her. He thought she was beautiful. To mean he understood why Ghost dug her, but he found her voice a bit annoying and kept wondering if she was real. Did she really believe all the chat she incessantly chatted? She was a walking contradiction. She dressed like a Kardashian but talked like the Winans.

"Bennie, Benny Wabasha," he said after a short deliberation.

"What's your middle name? Everybody has a middle name. You can tell a lot from a person's middle name. Well, not about the person more about the mother. What type of life she thought, they would have, or she wanted them to have, or what type of person she thought they would be."

This is a bunch of bullshit he thought, but I will play along, "Eugene my middle name is Ujjain. What does that tell you about my mother?" he said kind of sarcastically.

It didn't go missed. She shot him an awkward glance that made him smile. Then she asked, "How do you spell it?"

That was the tricky part his mother spelled his middle name Ujjain. He hated it because people always had questions, and he would have to explain. He wanted to lie, but instead, he spelled it.

"That's cute," she said surprising him. "Benny Ujjain the spelling is unique, but the name is common she thought you would be a leader. She gave you a name that is common, but a spelling that distinguishes you. She thought you would be a part of history and Benny...Benny is a good friend."

He never imagined himself making history and even in that glee resisted the temptation of telling her how right she was about him being a good friend. Instead, he just said, "Hum."

"Benny Ujjain Wabasha that's a strong name."

Benny began to feel a bit embarrassed and did something he had never done before; he blushed. There was something very disarming about her charm. They laughed through a mouthful of topics he didn't know how they got on the subject of God.

"If I died and he was standing there, I wouldn't be surprised, but I don't ask him for anything" Benny threw into the conversation.

"What about forgiveness?"

"I never do anything I am sorry about."

"It's not what you done that you disapprove but if you have done anything he might disapprove of." Benny thought for a moment.

"What makes you believe?"

"I feel him."

He looked at her curiously, and she thought it was funny.

"Not now dummy," she laughed, "but I can teach you."

He approached it lightly like he did the name game.

"First God doesn't do filth, so if you have done anything that you should feel guilty about you need to ask forgiveness."

Benny smiled at her, "That might take some time,"

Her demeanor stiffened, "You have to be serious." Before he could think, she took his hands and was praying. While wondering what he was doing with this girl, he thought about the preacher he didn't mean to kill, but he did. If he would have left it alone like Ghost had said, the preacher would be alive today.

Someday he knew he would have to talk to the lord about that. Being a Realist in the new sense of the word, he recognized if he was in front of the Lord it was as good a time as any. And the truth was, he was sorry. So as quietly as he possibly could, he said, "I am sorry." He thought about the guys in Lafontaine, but he didn't feel sorry for that. They were pressing that woman for her husband's debt. If he was wrong about that, he felt God would just have to tell him so.

"You said in your word, the Bible, that if two were

gathered together in your name, that you would be there. Here we are gathered praying Dear heavenly father because Benny wants to know you." Benny thought that was too strong of a statement when she added, "We pray you make your presence known to him." Just then the guys burst into the room. Benny Wu jumped and hollered, "Oh shit!"

Ghost looked confused, but Benny Wu being his friend he was fain to laughter.

Benny Wu pointed to Felicia, "You need to marry that one."

Ghost crossed the room looking between them. He grabbed Felicia's hands and softly pulled her to him, "I plan to."

She kissed him on the cheek and said, "Both of Y'all can slow down, let's see how we do at this party."

CHAPTER 14

"And the cracks began to show."

The party was Denny Ray's. If there was a place, Denny Ray shined it was in shining. Cappin' the art of showing off comes naturally to some. Denny Ray was one of those little boys who always wanted you to notice what they have. When he got new shoes he would walk with his feet sticking out, so you had to see them. ON TOP OF THAT he was a Scott. Third generation hood money, if the Scott's didn't know anything else, they knew how to throw a party.

Now honestly, there are only two things you need to throw a killer party, liquor, and a damn good DJ. Denny Ray put B.Y.O.D on the flyer. Rented the hall and put the rest of the money on the DJ, and booked DJ Lay.

Lay was a legend in Acres Homes Hip Hop. He was at the beginning of the movement. For over a decade his mix CD's were among the hottest in the city. Everyone in Houston has a DJ Lay CD in their collection, but that wasn't the reason he wanted Lay. Dj Lay was known for his old-school new-school remixes. Denny Ray's uncle was a major player. Lay did all of his events, and would always burn a CD of the hottest songs he played and a special old-school new-school mix just for that event.

"You know son your uncle pays extra for all of that."

"I don't give a damn what it cost." Denny Ray said as Lay eyes widen. "That's what I want." Denny Ray looked around the main hall of The Wreck.

The Wreck was a banquet hall that sat next to The Blue House on Mayview. They didn't rent it out for high school parties, but Ghost was able to get it because of his mother.

Denny Ray pointed toward the sliding glass doors to the backyard and said, "And I know a bunch of hot hoes. So I want them foam blowers you used at my uncle's bachelor party, I want them set up outside. That won't mess up them folk's grass will it?"

"It's biodegradable, nontoxic, won't even stain your clothes. Don't worry Son; I got you."

"I want you to make us look big Lay."

"Denny Ray" it was the first time Lay called him by his name, "you gone pay big boy money. I am not fen na give you no Chucky Cheese party. I am gonna run three 60 inch flat screens set 'em up behind the DJ. They play videos live mixed from the turntables. I am gonna put one camera in the crowd. My partner Cas, I stanched him up out of the military wrote this program that automatically mixes the video for whatever is on the tables. But you don't have to worry with the mechanics of that. You just hired Static Entertainment. I am bringing everything and everybody. We are coming at them full media, youngster. That's full lights, foam blowers, and fog machines, pushing 50,000 watts out them Concert JBLs, What else you want?"

"I want it hot, Lay. I want it hot!"

"Son, it's 20,000 people on my phone, it's gone be hot if I have to ship in the heat."

Lay did not disappoint when they drove up the place was jumping. Everything was just like Denny Ray planned; security had coned off their parking in the front. Benny Wu let Lil Eggy drive his car. No one had seen it, because all that time he had kept it at Ghost's house. So when they all pulled up everyone outside went crazy. Like ants, they rushed inside to tell everyone. Some of the people inside spilled outside then made a bubble around them. In the frenzy Denny Ray had forgotten about their surprise until the photographer's flash started cutting through the night. He jumped a bit at the first flash, and then popped his collar, hunched his shoulders and slid into his smile. Exalted in the thought that nothing makes you look more important than other people taking your picture.

It was like they were movie stars. Since they paid like they were ballers on the rise, Lay gave them something special. They walked in on a mix of Doug E. Fresh's The Show with an underground version of Crew Love that Drake did when he auditioned for Rap-a-Lot.

Everything that night was perfect, until the girls from Lincoln city the projects on the west end of Acres Homes started dancing against the girls from Garden city the projects on the north end. Benny Wu lived on Ferguson Way naturally he bet on Garden City. Tanasha Denny Ray's gal was ride or die for the Bricks, so Denny Ray was betting on Lincoln City.

Neither of the groups had names, so some of the guys started to bet on Benny's 'hoes' and some bet on Denny's 'hoes.' When Felicia walked up and heard one of the guys referring to the young ladies as such, she was incensed.

"Benny Ujjain Wabasha, are you serious!"

Everyone's head snapped to her, including Benny Wu. No one had ever heard his government name. Chuckling their heads swung back to him. He was standing there feeling naked. It was like she had his clothes in her hands. She turned and walked away.

Benny Wu stood there stunned for a moment and then took off after her, but at the door, she ran into Ghost. He wanted to go to her but thought it would be best if he let Ghost handle it.

Normally, Benny Wu slept like he ate, in patches here and there as needed or as life allowed. It was Monday, since Friday he hadn't slept a wink. It was Felicia the way she said his name, Benny Ujjain Wabasha. It was like she singled him out, not from the crowd but in the universe. Her disappointment was profound it felt both, empty and black, but what bothered him the most was that he cared.

The entire school was a buzz! All day long, everyone was congratulating them on the party, Ghost on his girl, equal love for Benny Wu and his new whip. With all the ravings, it felt like a complete failure to both of them.

Though neither would say it, it was for the same reason, the girl. Everyone had a great time except her, and because she didn't, neither of them did.

They nodded and smiled to everyone else. What they said to each other was.

"Dude your girl is tripping. I don't have control over what somebody calls somebody."

"Man, if I was you, I wouldn't even worry about it."

What Benny really wanted to know was how mad was she and was she ok. Ghost, on the other hand, was more concerned, with Benny Wu's unsolicited emotions. He meant exactly what he said with some stank on it.

Benny Wu could sense Ghost's growing anxiety; he decided to skip their last class Government.

He had said that her storming off wasn't fair to Ghost, but he wanted vindication for himself as well.

He walked up to her door in Sheppard Park Terrace. The house was pristine. The yard perfectly manicured. He looked down the street, they all were. All of the houses were perfectly edged and blown clean. Some of them dotted with people doing varied things. He noticed it was a striking contrast from what he was used to. But what made it different was the common denominator. These were black people too.

He pushed the bell, and the door popped opened as if she was waiting. She grabbed him by the arm and pulled him inside.

"I am glad you are here you can give me a hand, but first I want you to meet my grandmother."

He was surprised. She had said she, and her grandmother didn't get along. It had been his experience when girls do not get along with their people, they run out of the house, but she was different. She insisted that he meet her grandmother. Not contrary to what she had said but because of it. There was civility between them; he wrestled to understand.

Her grandmother was neither approving nor disapproving, but definitely, he was being judged. So he straightened his shoulders and smiled.

"Young man would you like a seat?"

Everything was antique Victorian. Bright yellow and white, it was beautiful he thought as he looked around the room and said, "No."

"Excuse me," she said in that way that let him know she heard exactly what he said.

Not that he was a liar, but his first inclination was to say that he had a lot to do and should just get started. It would sound good and productive, and he could quickly get out of there. However, when he opened his mouth, I am nervous came out.

There was something about her that made him know the truth was the only way to go.

"Well, you can have a seat we don't eat people."

"He smiled and took the seat farthest from her. He meant it as a joke but was impressed when she laughed.

She like the young man, he was honest and smart. He popped up and stuck his hand out, "Benny Wabasha everybody calls me Benny Wu."

She grabbed his hand and looked up at Felicia.

Knowing she was a college professor, he was expecting her to ask him about his college plans. Ms. Brenda Fay had made him fill out some applications, but he had not thought about it for real. Still he was ready with his answer, but she went somewhere completely different.

Looking at Felicia, she asked him how long had he and Marcus been friends.

"Ah," Felicia sighed but as smart as Benny Wu was, that shot went over the bow.

The detective was in a precarious position. She had figured it out that Barry was dead and more than likely murdered. However, with nobody and no witnesses, she could not prove it. She needed to turn up the heat but couldn't apply any pressure because she had no probable cause. Her captain gave her one more chance. All she had to do was connect Marcus or his car to Louisiana at the time the suspect's bank account was emptied. The phone rang; she was back in the game.

Ghost was sitting in class when they came through the door. He knew they were the police. They were in plain clothes, he could not see the six-pointed stars under their coats, but he knew they were laws. Before they showed them to Ms. Dumont, before she pointed to the right-side third seat from the back, he knew. He was already standing when the heads of the class turned toward the back where he was. He felt like running, but there was no place to go. He picked up his stuff and walked to the front of the class as the final bell was ringing.

All Benny Wu wanted to say was he was sorry. However, it was hard because he didn't know what he had done. He thought he wanted her to feel better. That wasn't the truth either. Felicia felt fine, and he knew it. He wanted her to feel better, about him.

"I didn't tell those guys to call those girls that."

"You didn't tell them, not to. A man should respect a woman even if she doesn't have the sense to respect herself."

"Maybe you're right. Whatever, you just shouldn't hold it against Ghost."

He said trying to remind himself and to clarify for her why he was there.

"I am not holding anything against Marcus, just like I am not holding anything against you. A person's guilt convicts them."

Bennie's phone rang it was Ghost, "Man where are you?"

Benny We looked into Felicia's face and said, "Around the corner, what's up?"

Ghost told him about the deputies bringing him the summons, to be in court tomorrow, "I need you to go with me."

"You know how I am about courts but" Benny Wu said. He almost threw in an expletive but considered his company and simply added, "That's what's up. I'll be there in a few." He said and hung up the phone.

She wanted to ask him why he had lied to his friend. Why he didn't tell him, he was there. Instead, she asked why he didn't like court.

"I make people nervous. Court is the last place you want people to act like they are scared of you."

"First you don't make me nervous, not like that. I am definitely not afraid of you, a little disappointed with you."

"See there you go. How can you be disappointed in me?" he said genuinely confused and surprisingly concerned.

"Because you are smart enough to see thru the myths, your mother was right."

He had never heard that before. No one had ever said that his mother was right about anything, "What was she right about."

"You are a leader; you have all those kids following you, where? Where are you leading them?"

Black kids love to shine, Benny Wu thought that's why he let Lil Eggy drive to the party. The better he dressed Lil Eggy and them; the better bait they'd become, soon he would be off the front line altogether. Then he would focus on smash and grabs. No guns just hammers and gloves pick soft targets with little security, as long as they don't have any weapons or don't turn the hammers towards anyone. But to what end. That was the one thing he never thought about, the end.

He looked down at the campaign signs, and took the easy out, "oh I get it everybody has to be Barack, now."

He threw up his shoulders like it didn't matter and tried to walk out with his lie. She could tell she had upset him. Like a child, she had put too much on his plate for one setting, "That's not what I meant" but it was too late he had lost his appetite.

He was headed for the door, when she said, "Wait."

He stopped in his tracks.

"Before you go, I want to give you something." She left, went into the back bedroom. Then came back with a blue suit, "This was my father's you and he are about the same size. It was the first thing I noticed about you."

He felt odd. She was so good it was hard for him to believe she was serious. On the same sleeve, her conviction couldn't be taken as a joke.

"I have been telling myself for years I would take then to Blue Birds, but I haven't been able to work up the nerve. This will look nice on you…my father would say, 'if you want to win on a basketball court you must wear the right shoe, but to win in a court of law you wear the right suit'…now here is the deal" she handed him the suit and took his phone out of his hand at the same time.

The motion was so fluid when combined with her speech; he didn't notice she had it.

"You have to text me a picture of you in the suit."

"I don't have your num-be-r," he said as she was handing the phone back.

CHAPTER 15

"Hail Mary"

She put all her cards on the table, "Mr. Womacky I think the guy that robbed you, is the guy I should be looking for." She left out the part about the murder.

She went on to explain her situation, "I can't put this guy in a lineup because I don't have probable cause to arrest. I can't get his picture for a photo lineup because he is a minor with no priors. However, right now he is in that building, being emancipated. If you happen to see him in a public place and unprovoked pick him out of a crowd of people... for wasting my time and having me traipsing backward through Louisiana, I am going to arrest him on the spot.

This is Nora Radcliff; she is an assistant district attorney." The young lady put her hand out to Mr. Womacky but looked at her friend, "First, I am putting myself and my career on the line" then she turned to Mr. Womacky looking him in the face, "...Mr. Womacky, before we go any farther, has she shown you any pictures or given you any type of description, said anything that may in any way influence your recollection?"

"No, she hasn't," he said although he wished she could have. Then he wouldn't have had to come all this way. He was still in considerable pain. However, he had to know the truth. He had to know if Shelia was really connected. She owed him a great deal of money, but not enough to die behind. Still, he didn't want to walk away from it either. Not after the detective made it sound to him like, he had been robbed by some punk angry because his daddy was playing in his booty. He had to know the truth.

"No one could influence me. I remember the young man. Clearly, I would know him anywhere."

That's the thing about a suit, a suit makes everyone look respectable, and Benny Wu was in a good one. He was walking past them as he said that.

Felicia's wanting to see him in her father suit was fortunate, but her pairing it with her father's tie from Rice that was a blessing.

Up north they call Rice the Harvard of the south. Down south in Texas Harvard is where you go if you can't get into Rice.

When Benny Wu walked up to the bailiff, wearing the tie he mistakenly identified Benny Wu as a graduate and said, "This way councilor." He grabbed Benny Wu by the elbow a shoved him through the side door reserved for lawyers. Everyone's eyes were on Benny Wu as he walked to the first row where he was instructed to sit.

Judge Nijinsky was a kindly old man who became a judge because he enjoyed marrying people. When asked to take a photo he would smile as wide as the bride. While he loved the law, he felt that it was families that made America great. His duties in the servers of the law, he saw as a way of protecting the family. As such he approached with considerable loathing his duties like emancipation.

Now, normally a child is only expedited into adulthood when they are believed to have killed someone. No matter how bent on justice the community is, civility won't allow them to execute a child. Not to compromise the sleep of the good people, someone would be forced to drop the gavel and grow them up.

Ghost's predicament was a lot less grim as he was being emancipated for tax purposes. Texas law is very kind to people with money. By him being an orphaned land owner, he qualified for certain tax deferments.

Nevertheless, Judge Nijinsky approached Marcus's emancipation with a strange combination of optimism and dread. Knowing that many people never learn to plan past the fantasies of adolescents, he saw a unique opportunity in this situation he very seldom had. And made it a condition of the emancipation that Ghost writes an essay on what type of old man he plans to be, adding, "While I understand the economics of your situation. There is much more to being an adult, than the paying of your bills. Now my good friends here,"

He was referring to Pastor Walker and Roderick Paul, the accountant Pastor Walker hired to look over the financial affairs of the estate, " has assured me that you will remain in their counsel.

This can be a tumultuous time in a young life. I would urge you to not only seek their counsel but trust it."

As he went through the business of the court, he could not take his eyes off Benny Wu. With the election of the first black president imminent, it was next to impossible not to be curious about such a young, charismatic black attorney from his alma mater.

"Bailiff" Judge Nijinsky lean forward, "Have the young Counselor to approach the bench."

The bailiff walked over to Benny Wu, "Counselor, the judge would see you." Benny Wu heart nearly jumped out of his chest. 'Would see you' he thought, 'what kind of sentence is that'?

Everything was getting so formal he thought as he approached the bench.

"We have not been formally introduced. You know that's my alma mater," the judge said pointing to Benny Wu's tie.

Benny grabbed it and finally got it, why there had been such confusion. It was the tie.

"Sir there has been a mistake this isn't my tie. Well, it is mine. My…." He paused slightly remembering. Ghost was directly behind him, "friend girl gave it to me."

There was a slight chuckle in the court. Even Judge Nijinsky found his desire for technical proficiency amusing and smile as well.

"Son, what is your name?"

"My Name is Benny Wabasha."

It is perceived outside of the great state, that a lot of people are executed in Texas, and it's true. The tolerance for nonsense is very low, but if you look at it in ratios proportionate to size, it's not that many in a given area. When the Judge Nijinsky heard the name Wabasha bells went off.

Benny Wu heard them too, "Yes sir he was my father."

"If you have a moment I'd like to speak to you in my chambers." He stood up and looked at the bailiff. Who promptly stood and said, "Court is adjourned" as Nijinsky slapped the gavel. Everyone stood and began to leave, except Ghost.

Judge Nijinsky looked at Marcus and could see the worried-look young man, "He's not in any trouble I would just like to speak to him in private."

"It's cool Marcus," Benny said reassuring him. Using Ghost's real name almost made both of them burst into laughter. "I'll meet you at the house."

CHAPTER 16

"Fear chose her paramour."

It may have seemed that Ghost was walking directly up to Detective DeValo and them. However, the shortest distance between any two points is a straight line, and they were standing directly between him and the flask of Belvedere he kept in the glove compartment now. While he was headed straight to his drink, his mind was on Benny Wu and the suit, that neither Benny Wu nor Felicia mentioned. He was sure that it didn't mean anything.

However, there was that thing his mother use to say, "A secret is just a lie in its fetal stage."

Preoccupied with that thought he had not noticed Detective DeValo until he was nearly on top of her. When he saw her, he was startled, but as was his character, he maintained composure and gave her a half smile. He wanted to walk pass them, but he overheard Detective DeValo.

Very seldom did she make a mistake but Mr. Womacky was her last chance. He was her master link. She had to prove that Ghost was in Louisiana when the money was withdrawn. She knew in her gut that Womacky's assault and the bank were connected. The same car that was caught on video by the bank was caught leaving Womacky's at the same time that he was robbed.

That next morning bright and early, someone withdrew all the money, and that same car drove pass the bank again. However, if she didn't make this connection, it was over. So when she realized Womacky didn't recognize Ghost, in her disappointment, she let her surrender slip and said, "Well that's, that."

To which Ghost naturally replied, "That's what?"

While she meant it was the end of this case. The end of her chasing ghosts, caring and possibly her career, what she intended to say was, "Nothing."

However, in the time it took her brain to have that thought and tell her mouth to make an N, Womacky had blurted out, "They thought you were the guy who robbed me."

"What?" Ghost replied his eyes questioning the group.

Detective DeValo tried to interrupt him, "Mr. Womacky."

"What? He's not the guy. The guy who robbed me was beefier; his teeth were whiter no offense."

Beefier with whiter teeth Ghost thought as he looked at the portly man on the crutches. Slowly it began to sink in who he was. He looked at Detective DeValo and smiled, they knew.

They knew about Barry, the murder, the money; they knew everything. His smile widened. It was just like Benny Wu had said, "No body, no witnesses, no murder."

His smile widened yet again then he trickled into a

soft, quiet giggle as he realized they couldn't prove anything!

They can't even prove that a crime happened at the bank. If they could Ghost reasoned there would be Feds all over the place. He looked all around. There were none. There was no one. Detective DeValo was alone except for this guy, who got robbed by somebody that was not him.

That was it; he burst into laughter. Everyone was a bit put off because it was obvious he was not laughing at Mr. Womacky's comment. His laughing turned into hurrahing. Soon he was behaving as if he had won The Masters. Bouncing up and down on the balls of his feet, with his fist balled tight. He brought them up across his chest and swung them down and hollered, "Woooo." Then exhaled loud was if he had been pulled from the water and could finally breathe.

There is no other word for it, it was selfish, but he knew he was clear.

Even if they arrested Benny Wu for robbery, they could hold his feet to the fire. Like his father, Benny Wu would take it to the needle. He looked at Mr. Womacky and said, "To answer your question. Sir, I don't give a damn." Then he was looking at Detective DeValo for whom he had no more words and walked off, chunking a peace sign in the air behind him.

Mr. Womacky was thinking what the hell is wrong with this fool when he noticed the ring. He knew the stone immediately. He opened his mouth to say so, but then on rethought figured he had better find out who this fool was, first. The guy who robbed him warned, "Don't make them send a fool, the next time they may start at Miss Ella May's."

Now that warning echoed in his mind. He wondered if this fool was the fool as he watched the seventeen-year-old kid walk to a $60,000 BMW, hop in and grab a flask out of the glove box. Then right in front of the courthouse take a huge swig.

Ghost wanted to call Benny Wu, but he knew Benny Wu's phone would be off in the courthouse and he couldn't go get him for fear he would lead them straight to him. So he did the only thing he could, he waited.

Now through the windshield, he and Mr. Womacky stared eye to eye. Ghost took a sip and thought about Detective DeValo. He had been watching her lips when she said his name. As he remembered, he mouthed the name with her, "Womacky" locking it into his recognition. Convinced he would never forget, he nodded his head and took another drink. Each time he tasted the liquor his mood deepened.

I know he is trying to take my gal, Ghost thought but then said softly to Womacky through the glass, "but you won't testify against him...Womacky." He pulled out his phone and took Womacky's picture.

The big man was already uneasy; when he saw the youngster take his picture, he moved on to worried. He was so consumed he was completely oblivious to the conversation going on just at his back.

Nora had pulled Detective DeValo by her sleeve, "Who is the new guy with Judge Nijinsky?"

Detective DeValo had never seen Benny Wu, but regardless her response would have been the same, "Nora Radcliff we are not in college; I don't know if you remember, but I am on a case."

146

"Nzingha," Nora called Detective DeValo by her sorority line name. Nzingha was the African queen, who would not have a King. Although she loved her line name, she didn't find the reference amusing.

Unconcerned with her disapproval Nora clarified, "I don't know if you were paying attention, but Mr. Womacky just told you that is not the guy. If you feel that strongly hand the case over to Homicide. Now I understand if you don't feel like playing, but I'm not married, and I do. If you're done, you can go. My car is over there." She pointed to her 450 CLS and then with the same hand beckoned and called to the judge.

She had to stretch and holler a bit. While they were close, they were still out of the range of bumping into each other. Hearing the Judge's name, Benny Wu's head snapped her way.

He noticed the beautiful young lady waving, but he recognized the back of Womacky immediately.

The first good look he got at Womacky it was from the back. Then like a coward, he was trying to run. Now he was staring through a car window at his best friend. DeValo had never seen Benny Wu, but he had watched her from the field across from Ghost's house. Seeing her with Womacky, he thought that she had put all of the pieces together. Ghost had obviously walked past her, so she didn't have anything on him, but then she couldn't. The only one, who could ever finger any of them, was him.

He knew they couldn't prove the murder because no one would ever find that pervert's body, and as far as the bank, there was no doubt he was clear. Turning the cameras off, whatever else Shelia did, it was to protect herself. He gave her the information, and she brought him the money minus $1500 that she said she had to give to one of the tellers. He never even went into the bank.

All they had was the assault, but that was enough to be afraid. Now most people as scared as Benny Wu was, would think flight. Just turn around and walk back into the courthouse and try to find another exit but Benny Wu embraced his fear. Instead of turning tail and running, he through his shoulders back and walked up to them.

Nora spoke first, "Hello Sir; I am Nora Radcliff the Assistant District Attorney out of the 313, Pamela Harrison's court. I just wanted to introduce myself." She was talking to the judge, but her eyes kept darting to Benny Wu, who was in a very dark place.

Benny Wu was watching Detective DeValo. He was waiting for her to make her move while he contemplated time. How much they would give him, or how much would he accept? How would he spend it? And there was the thing about having to do it in Louisiana.

He shifted his gaze to Womacky. Benny Wu wanted to be looking in his eyes when he picked him out. He noticed neither Nora's eyes, darting and flirting nor her smile screaming for his attention.

However, the judge did. He smiled and said, "Hi, Ms. Radcliff it's nice to meet you." He stuck his hand out and shook hers. Then put his arm around Benny Wu to pull him into the conversation, "and this is Benny Wabasha. We are expecting great things from this young man."

When the judge grabbed Benny Wu, it surprised him shockingly. The physical contact combined with his smiling, all warm and, promising. Benny Wu thought this is what Santa would look like without his beard and smiled back, for a moment forgetting his fate.

"That sounds very encouraging, coming from you Sir." Benny Wu said cheerfully to the kindly judge as he extended his hand to Nora, "It's nice to meet you, Ms. Radcliff."

It is funny how thoughts are linked. She was standing there, drinking him in. He was finding a little pleasure in her thirst. Something about her smile made him think about Felecia. That made him think about Ghost which reminded him that his best friend was sitting in the parking lot just a few feet away watching Womacky, and there we go.

He took a deep breath and prepared himself. He dropped his head and closed his eyes. He knew when he looked up and opened his eyes, he would see Womacky pointing at him, and DeValo would be pulling out her cuffs. He exhaled and opened his eyes, and there he was, Womacky, but he wasn't pointing. He was laying on the ground writhen in pain. Frighten almost out of his mind. The word homicide had gotten caught in his brain, and when he finally turned around to investigate, he saw his attacker shaking hands with the prosecutor. He was so frightened he had tried to run forgetting he was on crutches. He took a step and a half and crashed to the pavement.

Once again, Benny Wu pounced on him, but this time it was to help him, but Womacky was so terrified when Benny Wu touched him he messed himself.

Womacky got his answer. He had wondered if Shelia was connected, he turned to see her muscle being embraced by the judge. There was that fool in the parking lot and looks like the Assistant District Attorney might be in on it too. His imagination was running wild with the different ways they could be connected and how high and wide this thing could run. What have I gotten myself into, he thought? His mind was swirling as he tried to find a way out, while Bennie's untwisted and his became clear. However, first, he would have to calm Womacky down. This wasn't going to be easy because Womacky was so frightened he wouldn't even look at Benny Wu. He didn't want to say that he had seen him, ever, not even now.

That was it Womacky thought, my way out, "I haven't seen him," he mumbled. His head popped up, and he stared at the judge terrified. His smile twisted in fear and trepidation. In his voice, a trembling that pleaded for their lives, "I told her I didn't see him." That plea being everything he had he dropped his head exhausted.

Womacky felt as if he had limped into a nest of hornets. He looked down at the hand holding him and saw the ring, and just as clearly saw his mother's house being burned to the ground, with her and his son inside.

"It's ok, Sir." Benny Wu said. He was careful not to use Womacky's name since supposedly they had not been introduced. He continued, "No one is going to punish you because you didn't see some guy." Benny Wu hunched his shoulders and looked up at the others throwing his hand up as if he didn't know the guy they were talking about.

The fear and pain were so great Womacky became numb. Bennie's words were like a far away whisper, but he turned his head slowly towards the sound. Tracking into his view was Benny Wu.

"Look at me." Benny Wu said it again, "Look at me!"

Looking him in his eyes Benny Wu said, "You have my word this is ok."

Womacky was hungry to believe, so Benny Wu

continued to feed him, "I'm sure they appreciate everything that you have done, but it's time you looked after your own health. Do you understand?"

Benny Wu shook his head up and down, and Womacky did so in kind. Convinced that Womacky would keep quiet, Benny Wu concluded, "I know your doctor told you to take it easy. You go on and go home, sit down somewhere be quiet and get some rest."

CHAPTER 17

"The strength of the alchemist."

For a week, Benny Wu watched the front of his house, under his clothes he wore all white, his boxers, socks, and his shirt, a simple form-fitting, plain white T-shirt with no logos or tags, and he waited for the police, but they never came. All that time he stayed in contemplation not of the time but of the stain.

What would it mean to be a convicted felon in this new world? What would Felicia think? The way she acted at the party; what if she found out that the ring, she was giving him so much love for was stolen? She wasn't like the others.

If he told Pink that he had busted some dude over the head and jacked him for it, she would kiss it and tell him how sexy it looked on his hand, but Felicia, would more than likely never speak to him again.

That was the other thing. Why would that matter?

He thought back to the first conversation. They were talking about love. She was saying that she did not believe in unconditional love, "you show me someone exercising an

unconditional love I will show you someone being used."
He was impressed because, in his father's book,
unconditional love is listed as the cornerstone of pimping.
There was an entire section praising Tupac for taking a card
once reserved for the clergy and making it playable to the
masses.

Of course, her reasons were religious. She had gone
on a rant, about how in 1 Corinthians 13, the word charity in
the King James Version of the Bible was changed into the
word love in the New Standard Translation.

To Benny like many, it was no big deal, but she was
passionate. She explained that charity had no expectations.
That love even if not reciprocated bares a responsibility,
adding that God did not sacrifice his son out of charity it
was love. "I have never given my love to anyone," she
concluded "but when I do you can believe there will be
some conditions."

It bothered Benny how much he thought about
Felicia, not what she was but who she was. Okay, she was
beautiful and ungodly fine and that was dancing on his
psyche, but it was who she was.

He kept telling himself; she didn't matter. She like
this election didn't matter but like with her, he wondered
what it would be, and what would it mean? So he went more
out of curiosity than concern. A burning beating breathing
curiosity, he had to see; maybe he would see her. He would
not say it out loud. He was careful to only think it in shallow
thoughts, but he wanted to see her.

He expected there to be throngs of people. Like a
scene out of a civil rights movie. Orderly lines that stretched
around the corner and a police presence, T-shirt vendors the
whole nine. He might even see the Boudin-Man pull-up

with those smoked and spicy links. It is hard to go to an event in Acres Homes you don't see his truck whip up. If there are too many cars parked in the front of your house here, he comes.

However, when Benny pulled up, it was quiet. There were signs everywhere and a few volunteers, sitting around the mouth of the gate, but there weren't any other people in sight. There were no T-shirt sellers, no Boudin-Man, nothing; the streets were so quiet it felt like church.

He blew pass the volunteers, walked into the building, surely inside there would be crowds of people. He went inside the building that had been his elementary school, A.B. Anderson and found the machines lay empty.

For a moment, he began to believe that the people had let Obama down. That black folks were even sorrier than he thought. Then he saw this elderly old lady smiling. She was standing there with her hands clasped barely moving; at the same time, she was rocking in her joy. Then Benny realized that either this was a testimony to all of those volunteers or to the resolve of black folks, but everyone already voted.

He stood there in silence. The elderly lady, who had been watching, walked across the room to him. Her heels were making a clicking sound as they struck against the marble school floor. Watching her, he thought about Felicia, wondering what type of old lady she would be.

"Can I help you?" she asked.

"No I just wanted to see."

"It's a beautiful thing isn't it?"

Benny Wu nodded and said, "Yes madam I guess so."

She was old and looked as if she had been waiting

for this day her whole life. Her enthusiasm was bubbling, effervescently, and it was contagious. She smiled, and he smiled. Then she grabbed his hand to shake it, "You know you could be president someday."

People had said that to him before, all of his life, but there was something different in the old lady's eyes. She believed it. He wondered, what was that thing she saw? Was it the same thing Felicia saw? That thing his mother had hope for when she named him.

Others had said the same thing, but they were lying through their teeth. He knew they didn't see his little dusty ass as president or anything else. For most people, all he had been was more work. Another brick on their load and none of them ever saw him as anything other than that.

Even so, in this old lady, hope had been marinating. Her eyes were filled with such joy and adoration it was overwhelming. So much so he wanted to pull his hand away, but the old lady had it.

He viewed love as a commodity. All his life he had seen it bartered and traded.

Addiction being the only thing he feared. He treated love as if it were a drug, avoiding it like the plague, not realizing that he was already infected. He was addicted at birth.

He had run through life thinking that the key was not to love, but the trap of love is not that we love; the trap of love is the need to be loved.

But it was too late. He was caught, however snared he understood, for the first time completely, his mother, and father, why God created men in the first place. He remembered people saying, "God is love" but he never heard anyone say God created love.

What God said was "I will know you love me if you follow my commandments." but God never made any man love him. Verily he stands at the door a knocks. By giving man free will, God placed himself under a burden. Even God would have to be worthy of love.

He pulled his hand from her and said thank you and quickly shuffled out of the building.

Outside there was a Hispanic man on a tricycle selling ice cream. He looked at the weathered man and thought about his father, and the book, to thy own self be true. That is what his father wanted; more than anything, for him to be true to himself.

It was in front of him; it was behind him. The world was changing, he was changing. He had tried to ignore it, but Ghost was changing too. What that woman had in her eyes is what he wanted from Felicia. And it frightened him to think that's what he wanted from the world.